OVID

The Essential
METAMORPHOSES

OVID

The Essential
METAMORPHOSES

Translated and Edited by Stanley Lombardo
Introduction by W. R. Johnson

Hackett Publishing Company, Inc.
Indianapolis/Cambridge

15 14 13 12 11   1 2 3 4 5 6 7

For further information, please address:
  Hackett Publishing Company, Inc.
  P.O. Box 44937
  Indianapolis, IN   46244-0937

  www.hackettpublishing.com

Cover design by Brian Rak and Abigail Coyle
Text design by Elizabeth L. Wilson and Meera Dash
Composition by Agnew's, Inc.
Printed at Edwards Brothers, Inc.

Library of Congress Cataloging-in-Publication Data

Ovid, 43 B.C.–17 or 18 A.D.
 [Metamorphoses. English Selections]
 The essential Metamorphoses / Ovid ; translated and edited by Stanley
Lombardo ; introduction by W. R. Johnson.
  p. cm.
 Includes bibliographical references.
 ISBN 978-1-60384-624-0 (pbk.) — ISBN 978-1-60384-625-7 (cloth)
 1. Fables, Latin—Translations into English. 2. Metamorphosis—Mythology—
Poetry. 3. Mythology, Classical—Poetry. I. Lombardo, Stanley, 1943– II. Title.
 PA6522.M2L66 2011
 873'.01—dc22   2011016045

Contents

Detailed Table of Contents

Introduction

The History of Everything

Who among Ovid's first readers could have predicted that this master of numerous short comic poems, just at the midpoint of his poetic career, would undertake and complete a long and complex poem that would come to rival the *Aeneid* (and perhaps outdo it) in its influence on the literature of Western Europe? He had begun with publishing five volumes of lighthearted love elegies (later harshly winnowed and reduced to three volumes). He had then turned to witty, sometimes poignant representations of legendary ladies writing letters to the men who had absented themselves from their felicity (the *Heroides*). After this splendid compilation, he had written a poem in three volumes, giving cynical and shamelessly sexist (and hilarious) advice to men who needed help in obtaining the consent of the women they lusted after, the *Ars Amatoria,* a sort of seducer's manual. This poem (which may have earned him the intense displeasure of Emperor Augustus and his permanent exile to the Black Sea) was followed by the *Metamorphoses,* an immense poem in fifteen volumes, which took as its chief theme a paradox to which Heraclitus had given its essential form: "all things flow," "you never step into the same river twice"—in short, it is changing realities that constitute the only real permanence in the universe.

Ovid may have been drawn to this particular theme because it gave him warrant to retell stories that he happened to like, stories drawn from Greek myths that focused on (and explained) how given entities came into existence, in particular how certain beings, both semidivine and human, were transformed into animals, vegetables, and minerals. This seemingly limitless source, a narratological paradise, offered the storyteller all the material he needed to construct vivid characters, dramatic conflicts, and surprising outcomes. The major problem facing the poet who found this treasure house irresistible was how to impose on this delicious welter some semblance of intelligible order. (One of Ovid's masters, the Alexandrian poet Callimachus, had found a solution to this problem, but his *Aitia* [*The Origins*] exists for us only in fragments, and we have no real notion of how much help Ovid may have gotten from his great predecessor as he set about trying to devise a shape for, a pattern to, the tales of transfigurations he wanted to narrate.)

Ovid found the answer to his problem in history. To be more precise, in the history of the time he was living in. Like most of his contemporary inhabitants of the Mediterranean world, he felt that he was living at a moment of *weltwende,* of radical change in the world's destiny. Seventeen years before he was born, Julius Caesar had begun his conquest of Gaul and was preparing to invade Britain; six years before he was born, just as the Roman republic entered upon its implosion, Julius Caesar crossed the Rubicon and began his struggle to secure for himself absolute control of Rome; finally, in the year in which Ovid donned the toga of manhood (30 BCE), Octavian, Caesar's heir, defeated Antony and Cleopatra and was well on his way to becoming emperor of the Roman Empire. The nature of these events and the metamorphosis of Rome's political, economic, and military institutions they produced were quickly understood by some and gradually understood by everyone living in the Roman Empire.

But a writer born in the generation before Ovid's, Diodorus of Sicily, undertook to provide a remarkable representation of that knowledge and the feelings that it engendered. He wrote a universal history of the known world, beginning with the Middle East and India, going down through the Trojan War and the history of Greece to Caesar's invasions of Gaul and Britain. Substantial portions of his work remain, but much of it is fragmentary. We can surmise from his preface however that he was convinced that the successes of Julius Caesar—he was writing his history during the early years of Octavian-Augustus' reign—had marked a significant alteration in the history of the (known) world. It is perhaps not too much to say that he saw the history of the nations that he examined as being elements in a progression leading to the establishment of Rome's permanent hegemony or that he felt (he would not be alone in the feeling) that Caesar and Augustus had between them saved the world from its long zigzag patterns of law and disorder: there broods over Diodorus' preface a sort of intuition that what he and his first readers are witnessing is the end of history. That sense of a triumphant finale for history and its nations, one provided by Augustus and his role model, provides the frame for Ovid's great counter-epic. Augustus is emphatically (and wittily) alluded to early on in Book 1, and he and Julius put in a sudden and splendid joint appearance at the very end of Book 15. But before turning to these passages and the ironic world-historical frame they impose on Ovid's diverse and disparate tales of mutability and impermanence, it might be well to see how Ovid begins his poem.

Ovid's Cosmology

Unlike Diodorus, Ovid does not begin with Egypt and other ancient civilizations. Instead, like Hesiod's *Theogony*, he begins with Chaos, but he replaces Hesiod's primeval Void with a vision of the world's origins that smacks of something like atomic theory. Ovid's Chaos is "a crude, unsorted mass, / Nothing but an inert lump, the concentrated / Discordant seeds of disconnected entities" (1.7–9). This unpromising mess is gradually transformed into ordered entities by "Some god, or superior nature" (1.21), whichever god it was "who had sorted out this cosmic heap" and "divided it into parts" (1.32–33). We are here near the realm of Spinoza's *Deus sive Natura,* God or Nature. This god that is nature or this nature that is god is as much a product of the scientific imagination as it is of metaphysical speculation. The purpose of this surprising fusion of Epicurus' world-constituting atoms and the all-pervasive, all-governing god of the Stoics is to remove the true matrix of Ovid's stories from their usual playground, the one that Hesiod and Homer combine to design when they give Zeus (in this poem Jupiter) and his Olympians their permanent poetic identities. Jupiter and his Olympians will indeed dominate many of the stories in the first two-thirds of the *Metamorphoses,* but the poem and its stories is not about them. It is rather about the world in which human beings live and love and suffer. In initiating his poem in a space-time outside the realm of religious mythology that the stories he retells inevitably inhabit, Ovid makes clear that this is going to be a poem about nature and her progeny—even if the exact means by which the human beings who enact Ovid's stories come into existence is uncertain:

> Man was born, whether fashioned from immortal seed
> By the Master Artisan who made this better world,
> Or whether Earth, newly parted from Aether above
> And still bearing some seeds of her cousin Sky,
> Was mixed with rainwater by Titan Prometheus
> And molded into the image of the omnipotent gods.
> And while other animals look on all fours at the ground
> He gave to humans an upturned face, and told them to lift
> Their eyes to the stars. And so Earth, just now barren,
> A wilderness without form, was changed and made over,
> Dressing herself in the unfamiliar figures of men.
>
> (1.79–89)

The awkward and no doubt vexatiously intended mythological linking of Epicurus (seen here in the world's shared material substance, down to the divine seed from which humans are fashioned) and the Stoics (seen here in the gods who govern all, down to the orientation of the human face) gains in a provocative indeterminacy what it loses in clarity. But in this passage the two strains of thought conspire to provide nature (here Earth) and humankind (in its noblest aspect) with a unity that can be seen independently of the traditional mythologies that religion and politics nourish and depend on.

Heaven's King and His Earthly Double

Having accounted for the world and the creatures in it, the poet now turns to the description of the early history of humans: the Four Ages—Gold, Silver, Bronze, and Iron. The happy Golden Age is ruled over by Jupiter's father, Saturn, but "after Saturn was consigned to Tartarus' gloom / The world was under Jove, and the Silver race came in" (1.115–16). This means that the stories that make up the poem, from this moment on, take place in the Iron Age over which Jupiter holds dominion.

The first challenge Jupiter must deal with is the rebellious Giants, whom he easily defeats. In retaliation, Mother Earth creates a race of violent humans from their blood, and this "incarnation," which "also was contemptuous / Of the gods" (1.164–65) makes Jupiter very angry, so angry that he summons a council of the gods. Unlike Hesiod, his chief model up to this point, the poet does not relate how Saturn had seized power from his own father (Uranus) just as he has had his power wrested from him by his own son. By representing the creation of humans and their early history (the Four Ages) in such detail and by very briefly sketching Jupiter's seizure of power in a couple of verses, Ovid avoids explaining how Jupiter and his fellow Olympians came to possess the immense power they will wield throughout the rest of the poem. In doing so he avoids implicitly dwelling not only on Rome's implosion as a republic, its rise to empire, and its bloody history of civil war but also on the Olympians' earthly counterparts themselves. But the angry entrance of the king of Olympus into the poem creates a different and disturbing impression. Still irate with the Giants and now furious with their replacement (and doubtless with Earth who had given birth to all of his recent enemies), Jupiter summons a council of the gods and lays bare his plan to destroy mankind (1.186–203). The Olympian gods hasten by way of the Milky Way "to the royal palace / Of the great Thunderer" (1.174–75). The lesser (plebeian) gods live elsewhere, "but the great / All have their homes along this avenue. This quarter, / If I may say so, is high heaven's Palatine" (1.178–80). Ovid's blasphemous (and witty) equation of Olympus with the Palatine where Augustus lives is hardly mitigated by the ostentatious timidity of Ovid's "if I may say so."

Jupiter's is not a constitutional monarchy, and the council of the gods has not been summoned to debate or to advise. Nevertheless, when Jupiter singles out "infamous Lycaon" (1.203) as the worst of the humans whom he intends to destroy, the gods instantly demand his death.

> So it was when a disloyal few
> Were mad to blot out Rome with Caesar's blood,
> And the human race was stunned with fear of ruin
> And the whole world shuddered. The loyalty

> Of your subjects, Augustus, pleases you no less
> Than Jove was pleased.
>
> (1.205–10)

Here Augustus is formally identified as Jupiter's earthly counterpart, and these verses might, save for the wry irony that suffuses this passage, be reasonably judged as the copious flattery of a court poet. Some readers will decide against an ironic reading of this passage, but what cannot be denied is that the first story in the poem represents Augustus as Jupiter's human double and depicts Jupiter as a capricious tyrant, since despite what we have been told about those who live in the Iron Age, it is by no means clear that the majority of human beings are as wicked as Lycaon is purported to be, much less that all of humankind merits annihilation.

This emphatic linking of Jupiter and Augustus recurs in yet more spectacular form in the poem's final pages. When Ovid's history of everything that matters is almost complete, he concludes his poem with the apotheosis of Julius Caesar, whose supreme achievement, surpassing all his conquests and triumphs, turns out to be his having fathered the emperor Augustus: "For in all Caesar has done, / Nothing is greater than this, that he became / The father of our emperor" (15.834–36). Augustus, of course, was in fact the great-nephew of Julius, and Julius had only adopted him as his heir. But because Augustus has to be divine, it is necessary that his "father," Julius, be himself transformed into a divinity: "And so, that his son not have a mortal father, / It was necessary for Caesar to become a god" (15.846–47). When Venus realizes this, knowing that Julius, blood of her blood and her direct descendant, is about to be assassinated by his enemies on the Ides of March, she appeals to the other gods, but they are as helpless as she is against the decrees of the Fates. Then Jupiter calms and consoles his anguished daughter by revealing to her the splendid destiny that awaits her Roman progeny after Julius is murdered and deified (15.911–55). Once Julius has taken his fated place in heaven, his (adopted) son will perform his glorious deeds throughout the known world and, having gifted it with enduring peace, he will furnish it a model for morals, with an eye to its future, and he will pass on his name and reign to his stepson, Tiberius, and then follow Julius into godhood in the heavens:

And when peace has been bestowed on all these lands
He will turn his mind to the rights of citizens
And establish laws most just, and by his example
Guide the way men behave. Looking to the future
And generations to come, he will pass on his name
And his burdens as well to the son born to him
And to his chaste wife. And not until he is old
And his years equal his meritorious actions
Will he go to heaven and his familial stars.

(15.933–41)

Having finished this prophecy of Augustus' restoration of the
Golden Age, Jupiter instructs Venus to rush down to Rome and
snatch up the soul of dying Julius and bear it up to its heavenly des-
tination and final home. This she does, clutching it to her breast, but
its heat is such that she is forced to let go of it and it speeds off on
it own, traversing the sky as a glorious comet until it becomes a star.
It is from this vantage that Caesar comprehends the real meaning of
his former life on earth:

And now he sees
All his son's good deeds and confesses that
They are greater than his own, and he rejoices
To be surpassed by him. And though the son forbids
His own deeds to be ranked above his father's,
Fame, free and obedient to no one's command,
Puts him forward, only in this opposing his will.

(15.954–60)

So had Atreus yielded in glory to Agamemnon (a dubious compar-
ison), and Aegeus to Theseus, and Peleus to Achilles, and Saturn to
Jupiter. Jupiter reigns in heaven, and Augustus, surpassing his "fa-
ther," reigns on earth: "And as Jupiter is in control of high heaven /
And the realms of the triple world, the earth / Is under Augustus, as
both ruler and sire" (15.965–67). Having said so much, Ovid prays
to several of Rome's special guardian gods, those to whom a vatic
poet may offer his supplication, that after a long life on earth Au-
gustus may go to his heavenly reward and, once there, give ear to
the prayers of the Romans he left behind (15.968–80).

Once he has testified to the imminent divinity of Augustus in fulsome measure (deftly pilfering from Horace, *Odes* 2.20, 3.30), Ovid proceeds to claim deathlessness for himself, one that rivals the emperor's and in certain ways may surpass it (15.981–92). This immortality will be proof not only against fire, sword, and time but also against the anger of Jupiter. If, as seems as likely as not, this closing challenge to oblivion and power was composed after Ovid had arrived at his bleak destination on the Black Sea, he here underlines, again, his comparison of Augustus to Jupiter. In any case, thus far the poet has been right about both Augustus and himself. The emperor's influence on Western Europe and its various offspring is enduring if fragmentary. The poet's has been and continues to be as hardy as it is fertile. And his masterpiece, that strange omnium-gatherum of fragments, is whole and intact.

W. R. Johnson
University of Chicago

Note on the Text, Abridgment, and Introduction

This translation is based on G. P. Goold's revision of F. J. Miller's edition in the Loeb Classical Library series (1977). I have also consulted R. J. Tarrant's Oxford Classical Texts edition (2004) and adopted his readings in preference to Goold's in a number of instances.

The selections for this abridged edition were made with two audiences in mind: the general reader who wants to sample the most famous and influential tales in Ovid's *Metamorphoses* while gaining a sense of the whole, and the student in an undergraduate course in Greek and Roman mythology who will be reading a number of other texts.

Passages omitted from the poem's famously discontinuous narrative do not yield well to being represented by narrative bridges, as is typically done in an abridgment of a narrative work. The editing of the selections and the provision of what few headnotes are included in this abridgment thus aim primarily at making a selection comprehensible on its own terms rather than establishing continuity with what precedes it. A sense of the arc of the poem and its various subtexts should still be evident: the abridgment includes some fairly long bits of continuous text, including Book 1 in its entirety, selections from all but two books, and the poem's closing meditations on the course of Roman history. Omissions are signaled by ellipses (⋆ ⋆ ⋆), though most discontinuities in the text will also be clear from the line numbers, which are in almost all instances those of the unabridged translation from which the selections are drawn, the translator's *Ovid: Metamorphoses* (Indianapolis: Hackett Publishing Company, 2010).

In a handful of instances at the beginning of a selection, minor revisions to the translation as it appears in the unabridged edition have been introduced in the abridgment for the sake of clarity. Of course the headnotes, which are bracketed, have no authority in the Latin text of the poem.

Readers interested in a fuller treatment of the themes of the poem than is provided in the Introduction to this volume are directed to the Introduction to the unabridged translation noted above, of which the Introduction to this volume is an abridgment.

Suggestions for Further Reading

Barkan, Leonard. *The Gods Made Flesh: Metamorphosis and the Pursuit of Paganism.* New Haven: Yale University Press, 1981.

Bate, Jonathan. *Shakespeare and Ovid.* Oxford: Oxford University Press, 1993.

Brown, Sarah Annes. *The Metamorphosis of Ovid: From Chaucer to Ted Hughes.* New York: St. Martin's Press, 1999.

Du Rocher, Richard. *Milton and Ovid.* Ithaca: Cornell University Press, 1985.

Fantham, Elaine. *Ovid's Metamorphoses.* Oxford: Oxford University Press, 2004.

Forbes Irving, P. M. C. *Metamorphosis in Greek Myths.* New York: Oxford University Press, 1990.

Galinsky, Karl. *Ovid's* Metamorphoses: *An Introduction to the Basic Aspects.* Berkeley: University of California Press, 1975.

Hardie, Philip. *Ovid's Poetics of Illusion.* Cambridge: Cambridge University Press, 2002.

Hardie, Philip, ed. *The Cambridge Companion to Ovid.* Cambridge: Cambridge University Press, 2002.

Martin, Christopher, ed. *Ovid in English.* New York: Penguin, 1998.

Martindale, Charles, ed. *Ovid Renewed: Ovidian Influences on Literature and Art from the Middle Ages to the Twentieth Century.* Cambridge: Cambridge University Press, 1988.

Otis, Brooks. *Ovid as Epic Poet.* Cambridge: Cambridge University Press, 1970.

Segal, Charles. *Landscape in Ovid's Metamorphoses.* Wiesbaden: Franz Steiner Verlag, 1969.

Solodow, Joseph B. *The World of Ovid's* Metamorphoses. Chapel Hill: University of North Carolina Press, 1988.

Tissol, Garth. *The Face of Nature: Wit, Narrative and Cosmic Origin in Ovid's* Metamorphoses. Princeton: Princeton University Press, 1997.

Wheeler, Stephen M. *A Discourse of Wonders: Audience and Performance in Ovid's* Metamorphoses. Philadelphia: University of Pennsylvania Press, 1999.

Wilkinson, L. P. *Ovid Recalled.* Cambridge: Cambridge University Press, 1955.

Book 1

Invocation

My mind now turns to stories of bodies changed
Into new forms. O Gods, inspire my beginnings
(For you changed them too) and spin a poem that extends
From the world's first origins down to my own time.

Origin of the World

Before there was land or sea or overarching sky,
Nature's face was one throughout the universe,
Chaos as they call it: a crude, unsorted mass,
Nothing but an inert lump, the concentrated,
Discordant seeds of disconnected entities.
No Titan Sun as yet gave light to the world,　　　　　10
No Phoebe touched up her crescent horns by night,
Not yet did Earth hang nested in air, balanced
By her own weight, and Amphitrite had not yet
Stretched her arms around the world's long shores.
Yes, there was land around, and sea and air,
But land impossible to walk, unnavigable water,
Lightless air; nothing held its shape,
And each thing crowded the other out. In one body
Cold wrestled with hot, wet with dry,
Soft with hard, and weightless with heavy.　　　　　20

Some god, or superior nature, settled this conflict,
Splitting earth from heaven, sea from earth,
And the pure sky from the dense atmosphere.
After he carved these out from the murky mass,
In peaceful concord he bound each in its place.
The fiery, weightless energy of the convex sky
Shot to the zenith and made its home there.
The air, next in levity, was next in location,

Then the denser earth attracted the heavier elements
And was pushed down by her own weight. The circling sea   30
Settled down at her edges, confining the solid orb.

Then, the god who had sorted out this cosmic heap,
Whoever it was, and divided it into parts,
First rolled the earth, so it would not appear
Asymmetrical, into the shape of a great sphere;
And then he ordered the sea to flood and swell
Beneath high winds until it lapped the planet's shores.
He threw in springs and immense wetlands,
Lakes and rivers, which he channeled in sloping banks
So some are absorbed by the land itself, while others cascade   40
Into the sea, where received at last into open water
They beat no longer against banks but shores.
He also ordered the prairies to stretch, the valleys to sink,
The woods to take leaf, rocky mountains to rise.
And as two zones belt the sky on the right,
Two on the left, and a fifth burns in the middle,
This providential god marked the globe beneath
With these same five zones, so that of the earth's regions
The middle is too hot for habitation,
Deep snow covers two, but the two wedged between   50
Have a climate that tempers heat with cold.

Hanging above is the air, as much heavier
Than fire as water is lighter than earth.
The god ordained mist and clouds to form there,
And thunder that would make human minds tremble,
And winds too, gusting with thunder and lightning.
The World's Fabricator did not allow the winds
Free rein in the air. He barely controls them now,
When each must blow in his own tract of heaven,
Else they would shred the world with their fraternal strife.   60
Eurus receded to the East and the Nabataean realms,
To Persia and its ridges bathed in morning light.
Evening, and the shores warmed by the setting sun,
Are nearest to Zephyrus. Bristling Boreas
Invaded Scythia and the Arctic stars. The land

Due south drips with Auster's constant mist and rain.
Above all these he put the liquid, weightless
Aether, which has nothing of earthly dregs.

The deity had just finished zoning off everything
When the stars, which had long been smothered   70
In dark vapor, peeked out and glowed all over the sky.
And so that no region would be without living things
Of its own, constellations and the forms of gods
Possessed heaven's floor; the sea allowed itself
To swarm with glistening fish, the land became
A wild kingdom, and the air teemed with wings.

Still missing was a creature finer than these,
With a greater mind, one who could rule the rest:
Man was born, whether fashioned from immortal seed
By the Master Artisan who made this better world,   80
Or whether Earth, newly parted from Aether above
And still bearing some seeds of her cousin Sky,
Was mixed with rainwater by Titan Prometheus
And molded into the image of the omnipotent gods.
And while other animals look on all fours at the ground
He gave to humans an upturned face, and told them to lift
Their eyes to the stars. And so Earth, just now barren,
A wilderness without form, was changed and made over,
Dressing herself in the unfamiliar figures of men.

The Four Ages

Golden was the first age, a generation   90
That cultivated trust and righteousness
All on its own, without any laws, without fear
Or punishment. There were no threatening rules
Stamped on bronze tablets, no crowds of plaintiffs
Cowering before judges: no one needed protection.
Not a pine was cut from its native mountain
To be launched on a maritime tour of the world;
Mortal men knew no shores but their own.
Steep trenches around cities were still in the future;
There were no bronze bugles, no curved, blaring horns,   100

No helmets or swords. Without a military
A carefree people enjoyed a life of soft ease.
The inviolate earth, untouched by hoes, still
Unwounded by plows, bore fruit all on its own,
And content with food unforced by labor
Men gathered arbute, mountain strawberries,
Wild cherries, blackberries clinging to brambles,
And acorns that fell from Jove's spreading oaks.
Spring was eternal, and mild westerly breezes
Soughed among flowers sown from no seed.   110
Even uncultivated the soil soon bore crops
And fields unfallowed grew white with deep grain.
Rivers flowed with milk, streams ran with nectar,
And honey dripped tawny from the green holm oak.

After Saturn was consigned to Tartarus' gloom
The world was under Jove, and the Silver race came in,
Cheaper than gold but more precious than bronze.
Jupiter curtailed the old season of spring
And by adding cold and heat and autumn's changes
To a brief spring, made the year turn through its four seasons.   120
For the first time the air, parched and feverish,
Began to burn, and icicles now hung frozen in wind.
People now took shelter; their houses were caves,
Dense thickets, and branches bound together with bark.
Cereal seeds now lay buried, sown in long furrows,
And for the first time oxen groaned under the yoke.

The next and third generation was Bronze,
Harsher in its genius and more ready to arms,
Not wicked however.
                            The fourth and last is Iron.
Every iniquity burst out in this inferior age.   130
Shame and Veracity and Faith took flight,
And in their place came Duplicity and Fraud,
Treachery and Force, and unholy Greed.
They spread sails to the winds still a mystery
To sailors, and keels that once stood high in the mountains
Now surged and bucked in unfamiliar waves.

The cautious surveyor now marks off the fields
Once held in common like the sunlight and air.
And the rich earth is not only required to produce
Crops and food: now her bowels are tunneled,   140
And the ore she'd sequestered in Stygian darkness
Is now dug up as wealth that incites men to crime.
Iron with its injuries and more injurious gold
Now came forth, and War, equipped with both of these metals,
Brandishes clashing weapons in bloodstained hands.
Plunder sustains life; guest is not safe from host,
Or a father safe from his daughter's husband;
Gratitude is rare even among brothers. Husbands
Can't wait for their wives to die, wives reciprocate,
Frightful stepmothers brew their aconite, and sons   150
Inquire prematurely into their father's age.
Piety lies beaten, and when the other gods are gone,
Virgin Astraea abandons the bloodstained earth.

The Giants

And, so the lofty sky would not be safer than earth,
They say the Giants went after the kingdom of heaven,
Piling up mountains all the way to the stars.
Then the Father Almighty shattered Olympus
With a well-aimed thunderbolt and blasted away Pelion
From Ossa beneath. When the Giants' dread corpses
Lay crushed beneath their own bulk, they say Mother Earth,   160
Drenched with her sons' blood, reanimated
Their steaming gore, and to preserve the memory
Of her former brood, gave it a human form.
But this incarnation also was contemptuous
Of the gods, with a deep instinct for slaughter,
And violent. You could tell they were sons of blood.

The Council of the Gods

Jupiter, seeing this from his high throne, groaned.
He recalled, too, the sordid dinner parties of Lycaon,
Too recent for the story to be well-known, and conceived
In his heart a mighty wrath worthy of the soul of Jove.   170
He called a council, and none of the gods were late.

On a clear night you can see a road in the sky
Called the Milky Way, renowned for its white glow.
This is the road the gods take to the royal palace
Of the great Thunderer. To the right and the left
The halls of the divine nobility, doors flung open,
Are thronged with guests. The plebeian gods
Live in a different neighborhood, but the great
All have their homes along this avenue. This quarter,
If I may say so, is high heaven's Palatine.   180

So, when the gods had been seated in a marble chamber,
The God himself, enthroned high above the rest, leaning
On his ivory scepter, shook three times, four times,
The dread locks whereby he moves land, sea, and stars.
And opening his indignant lips, he spoke in this way:

"I was not more concerned than I am now
For the world when the serpentine Giants threatened
To get their hundred hands on the captured sky.
Although the enemy was brutal, that war at least
Stemmed from a united body and single source.   190
But now, wherever old Nereus' ocean roars,
The human race must be destroyed. By the river
That glides through the underworld grove of Styx,
I swear that I have already tried everything else,
But gangrenous flesh must be cut away with a knife
Before it infects the rest. I have demigods to protect
And rustic deities—nymphs, fauns, satyrs,
And sylvan spirits on the mountainsides.
Although we do not deem them worthy of heaven,
We should at least let them live in their allotted lands.   200
Do you think they will be safe there, I ask you,
When even against me, who rule you gods,
Snares are laid by the infamous Lycaon?"

The gods all trembled and zealously demanded
The traitor's head. So it was when a disloyal few
Were mad to blot out Rome with Caesar's blood,
And the human race was stunned with fear of ruin

And the whole world shuddered. The loyalty
Of your subjects, Augustus, pleases you no less
Than Jove was pleased. With word and gesture   210
He stilled the crowd, and when the clamor
Had been suppressed by his royal gravitas,
Jove once more broke the silence, saying:

"He has paid the penalty—of that you can be sure—
But listen to what he did, and hear his punishment.

Lycaon

The infamy of the age had reached my ears,
And hoping to discover the report was false, I slipped down
From Olympus, a god disguised as a human,
And crisscrossed the land. There is not time to do justice
To the catalog of iniquity I found everywhere.   220
The report fell short of the truth. I had traversed
Mount Maenala, its thickets bristling with animal lairs,
Crossed Cyllene, and Lycaeus' cold pine forests,
And was coming up to the Arcadian tyrant's
Inhospitable hall as the late evening shadows
Ushered in the night. I gave a sign that a god had come,
And the common people began to pray. Lycaon
Started by mocking their pieties, and then said,
'I'll find out if this is a mortal or a god. A simple test
Will establish the truth beyond any doubt.'   230
The test of truth he had in mind was to murder me
While I was fast asleep. And not content with that,
He slit the throat of a Molossian hostage,
Boiled some of his half-dead flesh and roasted the rest.
As soon as he set this delicate dish before me,
My avenging lightning brought down the house
On its master and his all-too-deserving household.
He fled in terror, and when he reached the silent fields
He let loose a howl. He tried to speak but could not.
His mouth foamed, and he turned his usual bloodlust   240
Against a flock of sheep, still relishing slaughter.
His clothes turned into a shaggy pelt, his arms into legs.
He became a wolf, but still retains some traces

Of his former looks. There is the same grey hair,
The same savage face; the same eyes gleam,
And the same overall sense of bestiality.
Only one house has fallen, yet more than one
Has deserved perdition. Erinys, the wild Fury,
Reigns supreme to the ends of the earth. You would think
They were sworn in blood to a life of crime! Let them all   250
Pay quickly the price they deserve—this is my edict."

Some of the gods voiced their approval and even
Goaded him on, while others playacted their silent consent,
But they all winced on the inside at the impending loss
Of the human race and wondered out loud
What the world would be without men. Who would bring
Incense to their altars? Was Jupiter planning
To deliver the world to the depredations of beasts?
The master of the universe told them to let him
Worry about all that, and he promised them a new race,   260
Different from the first, from a wondrous origin.

The Flood

He was poised to hurl volleys of thunderbolts
All over the world, but he backed off in sudden fear
That the conflagration might kindle the sacred aether
And set the long axis on fire from pole to pole.
He recalled, too, that a time was fated to come
When land and sea and heaven's majestic roof
Would catch fire, and the foundations of the world
Would go up in flames. So he laid aside
The weapons forged by Cyclopean hands   270
And chose instead a different punishment:
To overwhelm humanity with an endless deluge
Pouring down from every square inch of sky.

So he shut up the North Wind in Aeolus' cave
Along with every breeze that disperses clouds.
But he cut loose the South Wind, which scudded out
On dripping wings, scowling in pitch-black mist,

His beard sodden with rain, his white hair
Streaming water, clouds nesting on his forehead,
And dew glistening on all his feathers and robes.   280
The flat of his hand presses low-hanging clouds
And rain crashes down from the sky. Then Iris,
Juno's rainbowed messenger, draws up more water
To feed the lowering clouds. Crops farmers prayed for
Are beaten flat; years of hard work are all blotted out.

Jove's wrath was not content with his own sky's water,
So his sea-blue brother rolled out auxiliary waves.
The Rivers jumped to formation in their tyrant's palace
And he gave his command:
                         "My brief to you is to pour forth
Everything you have. This is a crisis. Open wide   290
Your doors and dikes and give your streams free rein!"

The Rivers returned, uncurbed their springs,
And tumbled unbridled down to the sea.

Neptune himself struck the Earth with his trident;
She trembled, and split mouths wide open for geysers,
And the Rivers spread out over the open plains,
Sweeping away orchards and crops, cattle and men,
Houses and shrines and the shrines' sacred objects.
If any houses were able to resist this disaster
And still stood, the waves soon covered their roofs,   300
And towers were submerged beneath the flood.
And now sea and land could not be distinguished.
All was sea, but it was a sea without shores.

Here's a man on a hilltop, and one in his curved skiff,
Rowing where just yesterday he plowed. Another one
Sails over acres of wheat or the roof of his farmhouse
Deep underwater. Here's someone catching a fish
In the top of an elm. Sometimes an anchor
Sticks in a green meadow, or keels brush the tops
Of vineyards beneath. Where slender goats once browsed   310

Seals now flop their misshapen bodies. Nereids gape
At houses, cities, and groves undersea,
And dolphins cruise through forest canopies,
Grazing the oak trees with their flippers and tails.
Wolves swim with sheep, tawny lions and tigers
Tread the same currents. The boar's lightning tusks
And the stag's speed are useless as the torrent
Sweeps them away. With no land in sight, no place to perch
The exhausted bird drops into the sea,
Whose unbridled license has buried the hills   320
And now pounds mountaintops with unfamiliar surf.
Most creatures drown. Those spared by the water
Finally succumb to slow starvation.

Deucalion and Pyrrha

Phocis is a land that separates Boeotia
From Oetaea, a fertile land while it was still land,
But now it was part of the sea, a great plain
Of flood water. There is a steep mountain there
With twin peaks stretching up through the clouds
To the high stars. Its name is Parnassus.
When Deucalion and his wife landed here   330
In their little skiff (water covered everything else)
They first paid a visit to the Corycian nymphs,
The mountain gods, and Themis, who was the oracle then.
There was no man better or more just than he,
And no woman revered the gods more than she.
When Jupiter saw the whole world reduced
To a stagnant pond, and from so many thousands
Only one man left, from so many thousands
Only one woman, each innocent, each reverent,
He parted the clouds, and when the North Wind   340
Had swept them away, he once again showed
The earth to the sky, and the heavens to the earth.
The sea's roiling anger subsided, as Neptune
Lay down his trident and soothed the waves. He hailed
Cerulean Triton rising over the crests,
His shoulders encrusted with purple shellfish,

And told him to blow his winding horn
To signal the floods and streams to withdraw.
Old Triton lifted the hollow, spiraling shell
Whose sound fills the shores on both sides of the world   350
When he gets his lungs into it out in mid-ocean.
When this horn touched the sea god's lips, streaming
With brine from his dripping beard, and sounded the retreat,
It was heard by all the waters of land and sea,
And all the waters that heard were held in check.
Now the sea had a shore, rivers flowed in channels,
The floods subsided, and hills emerged into view.
The land rose up; locales took shape as waters shrank,
And at long last the trees bared their leafy tops,
Foliage still spattered with mud left by the flood.   360

The world was restored. But when Deucalion saw
It was an empty world, steeped in desolate silence,
Tears welled up in his eyes as he said to Pyrrha,

"My wife and sister, the last woman alive,
Our common race, our family, our marriage bed
And now our perils themselves have united us.
In all the lands from sunrise to sunset
We two are the whole population; the sea holds the rest.
And our lives are far from guaranteed. These clouds
Still strike terror in my heart. Poor soul,   370
What would you feel like now if the Fates
Had taken me and left you behind? How could you bear
Your fear alone? Who would comfort your grief?
You can be sure that if the sea already held you,
I would follow you, my wife, beneath the sea.
Oh, if only I could restore the people of the world
By my father's arts, breathe life into molded clay!
Now the human race rests on the two of us.
We are, by the gods' will, the last of our kind."

He spoke and wept. Their best recourse was to implore   380
The divine, to beg for help through sacred prophecy.

So they went side by side to the stream of Cephisus,
Which, though not yet clear, flowed in its old banks.
They scooped up some water, sprinkled their heads and clothes,
And made their familiar way to the sacred shrine
Of the goddess. The gables were stained with slime and mold,
And the altars stood abandoned without any fires.
When they reached the temple steps, husband and wife
Prostrated themselves, kissed the cold stone trembling,
And said, "If divine hearts can be softened by prayers   390
Of the just, if the wrath of the gods can be deflected,
Tell us, O Themis, how our race can be restored,
And bring aid, O most mild one, to a world overwhelmed."

The goddess, moved, gave this oracular response:

"Leave this temple. Veil your heads, loosen your robes,
And throw behind your back your great mother's bones."

They stood there, dumbfounded. It was Pyrrha
Who finally broke the silence, refusing to obey
The commands of the goddess. She prays for pardon
With trembling lips, but trembles all over   400
At the thought of offending her mother's shades
By tossing her bones. Stalling for time,
The pair revisit the oracle's words, turning them
Over and over in their minds, searching out
Their dark secrets. At last Prometheus' son
Comforts the daughter of Epimetheus
With these soothing words:
                              "Either I'm mistaken
Or—since oracles are holy and never counsel evil—
Our great mother is Earth, and stones in her soil
Are the bones we are told to throw behind our backs."   410

Pyrrha was moved by her husband's surmise,
But the pair still were not sure that they trusted
The divine admonition. On the other hand,

What harm was there in trying? Down they go,
Veiling their heads, untying their robes, and throwing stones
Behind them just as the goddess had ordered.
And the stones began (who would believe it
Without the testimony of antiquity?)
To lose their hardness, slowly softening
And assuming shapes. When they had grown and taken on   420
A milder nature, a certain resemblance
To human form began to be discernible,
Not well defined, but like roughed-out statues.
The parts that were damp with earthy moisture
Became bodily flesh; the rigid parts became bones;
And the veins remained without being renamed.
In no time at all, by divine power, the stones
Thrown by the man's hand took the form of men
And from the woman's scattered stones women were born.
And so we are a tough breed, used to hard labor,   430
And we are living proof of our origin.

Earth herself spontaneously generated
Various other species of animals.
The sun warmed the moisture left from the flood,
Slime in the swamps swelled with the heat,
And seeds of life, nourished in that rich soil
As in a mother's womb, slowly gestated and took on
Distinctive forms. It was just as when the Nile,
With its seven mouths, withdraws from the flooded fields
Into its old channel, and then the Dog Star bakes   440
The plains of soft muck, and farmers turning over the clods
Find many animate things, some just on the verge
Of new life, some unfinished and just budding limbs,
And sometimes they see in the very same body
A part living and breathing, and a part still raw earth.
For when heat and moisture combine, they conceive,
And all things are born from their blended union.
And though fire fights water, moist vapor is fecund,
And this discordant concord is pregnant with life.

So when Mother Earth's diluvian mud   450
Again grew warm under the rays of the sun,
She brought forth innumerable species, restoring some
Of the ancient forms, and creating some new and strange.

Python

She would have rather not, but Earth begot you then,
O Python, greatest of serpents and never before seen,
And a terror to the new people, sprawling over
Half a mountainside. The god of the bent bow
Destroyed him with weapons never used before
Except against does and wild goats on the run,
Nearly emptying his quiver of arrows,   460
And venom oozed from the monster's black wounds.
And so Time would not tarnish the fame of this deed
He founded sacred games for the crowds, called Pythian
From the name of the serpent he had overcome.
Here every youth who won with his fists or his feet,
Or his chariot, received a garland of oak leaves.
There was no laurel yet, and Apollo wreathed
His brow and the gorgeous locks of his hair
With a garland from whatever species of tree.

Apollo and Daphne

Apollo's first love was Daphne, Peneus' daughter,   470
Not by blind chance but because Cupid was angry.
Flush with his victory over Python, the Delian god
Saw him stringing and flexing his bow, and said:

"What do you think you're doing, you little imp,
With a man's weapons? That archery set
Belongs on my shoulders. I can take dead aim
Against wild beasts, I can wound my enemies,
And just now I laid low in a shower of arrows
Swollen Python and left his noxious belly
Spread out over acres. You should be satisfied   480
With using your torch to inflame people with love
And stop laying claim to glory that is mine."

The son of Venus replied:
                    "Phoebus, your arrows
May hit everything else, but mine will hit you.
And as much as animals are inferior to gods,
So is my glory superior to yours."
                  He spoke
And, beating his wings with a vengeance, landed
On the shady peak of Parnassus. He stood there,
And drew from his quiver two quite different arrows,
One that dispels love and one that impels it.   490
The latter is golden with a sharp glistening point,
The former blunt with a shaft made of lead.
The god struck the nymph with arrow number two
And feathered the first deep into Apollo's marrow.

One now loved, the other fled love's very name,
Delighting in the deep woods, wearing the skins
Of animals she caught, modeling herself
On the virgin Diana, her tousled hair tied back.
She had many suitors but could not endure men,
So she turned them away, and roamed the pathless woods 500
Without a thought of Hymen, or Amor, or marriage.
Her father often said, "You owe me a son-in-law, girl."
Often observed, "You owe me grandchildren, my daughter."
But she hated the wedding torch like sin itself
And her beautiful face would blush with shame
As she hung from his neck with coaxing arms, saying,

"O Papa, please, won't you let me enjoy
My virginity forever? Diana's father let her."

Of course he agreed; but your very loveliness, Daphne,
Prevents your wish, your beauty opposes your prayer. 510

Apollo loves her at sight and desires to wed her.
What he desires he hopes for, but here his oracular
Powers desert him. As light stubble blazes
In a harvested field, or as a hedge catches fire

From embers a traveler has let get too close
Or has forgotten at daybreak, so too the god
Went up in flames, and all his heart burned
And fed his impossible passion with hope.
He sees the hair that flows all across her neck
And wonders, "What if it were combed?" Sees her eyes   520
Flash like stars; sees her mouth, which merely to see
Is hardly enough. He praises her fingers, her hands,
Her arms, which for the most part are bare,
And what is hidden he imagines is better.

Her flight is faster than if she were wind,
And she does not pause to hear him calling her back:

"Nymph of Peneus, I beg you, stop! I am not
Pursuing you as an enemy. Please, nymph, stop!
This is how a lamb runs away from a wolf,
A deer from a lion, a trembling dove from an eagle,   530
Each from her enemy, but Love makes me pursue you.
Ah, I am afraid you will fall, afraid that brambles
Will scratch your shins and that I, oh so wretched,
Will be the cause of your pain. This is rough terrain
You are running through. Run a little slower,
Please, and I'll slow down too. Or stop and ask
Who your lover is—no hillbilly or shepherd—
I don't mind the herds here, like some shaggy oaf.
You do not know, my rash one, you just don't know
Who you are running from, and that's why you run.   540
Delphi is mine; I am lord of Claros and Tenedos
And the realm of Patara. Jove is my father.
What shall be, what is now, and what has been
Are all revealed by me. It is through me that songs
Are played in tune on the lyre. My arrows are sure,
But one arrow more sure has wounded my heart
That once was carefree. I invented medicine,
I am called the Healer throughout the world,
The potency of herbs is my domain, but oh,

Love cannot be cured by herbs, and the arts   550
That benefit all are of no use to their lord."

He would have said more, but the Peneid nymph
Was running scared and left his words unfinished.
She was still a lovely sight. The wind bared her body
And as she cut through the air, her clothes fluttering
As her hair streamed out behind her in the breeze,
Her beauty augmented by flight. But the young god
Could not waste any more time on sweet talk,
Not with the Love God himself urging him on,
And he picked up the pace. A Gallic hound   560
Snuffs out and starts a hare in a field,
The hound running for prey, the hare for her life,
And now the hunter thinks he has her, thinks
Any moment now, his muzzle grazing her heels,
While she, unsure whether she is finally caught,
Writhes out of his jaws with a sudden spurt.
So too the virgin and the deity ran,
His speed spurred by hope and hers by fear,
But the pursuer closed in, boosted by Cupid's wings,
And he gave her no rest, staying right on her back,   570
His breath fanning the hair on the base of her neck.
She turned pale as her strength began to run out,
Beaten by the speed and the length of the race.
When she saw the waters of the Peneus, she cried,

"Help me, father! If your streams have divine power,
Destroy this too pleasing beauty of mine
By transforming me!"
                       She had just finished her prayer
When a heavy numbness invaded her body
And a sheathe of bark enclosed her soft breast.
Her hair turned into fluttering leaves, her arms   580
Into branches; her feet, once so swift,
Became mired in roots, and her face was lost
In the canopy. Only her beauty's sheen remained.

Apollo still loved her, and pressing his hand
Against her trunk he felt her heart quivering
Under the new bark. He embraced her limbs
With his own arms, and he kissed the wood,
But even the wood shrank from his kisses.
The god said to her:

      "Since you can't be my bride
You will be my tree. My hair will be wreathed   590
With you, Laurel, and you will crown my quiver and lyre.
You will accompany the Roman generals
When joyful voices ring out their triumphs
And their long parades wind beneath the Capitol.
You will ornament Augustus' doorposts,
A faithful guardian standing watch over
The oak leaves between them. And just as my head
With its unshorn hair is forever young,
You will always wear beautiful, undying leaves."

Apollo was done. The laurel bowed her new branches 600
And seemed to nod her leafy crown in assent.

Io

There is a gorge in Thessaly with steep wooded slopes
That men call Tempe. The foam-flecked water
Of the Peneus River tumbles through this valley
From the foot of Mount Pindus, and its heavy descent
Forms clouds that drive along billowing mist,
Sprinkles the treetops with spray and, cascading down,
Fills even the distant hills with its roar.
Here is the house, the abode, the inner sanctum
Of the great River. Seated here, in a cavern   610
Carved from boulders, he lays down the law
To his streams, and the nymphs who live in his streams.
The neighboring rivers convened here first,
Unsure whether to console or congratulate
Daphne's father. Spercheios came sporting poplars,
Restless Enipeus, old Apidanos,
Gentle Amphrysos, Aeas too, and soon all the streams,

Whatever wandering courses their weary waters
Take down to the sea. Only Inachus is absent.
Hidden deep in a cave, his stream swelling with tears,   620
He laments in his misery his lost daughter, Io,
Not knowing if she lives or is lost among the shades.
Finding her nowhere, he imagines her nowhere,
And in his heart he fears even worse.

                                        Jupiter
First laid eyes on her as she made her way
From her father's stream, and he said to her:

"Virgin worthy of Jove, clearly destined to make
Some man or other happy in your bed,
You should find some shade over there in the woods"
(Pointing) "while it is hot and the sun is high.   630
If you are afraid to go alone where the wild things live,
You can go with the safe protection of a god,
And no ordinary god either. I am the one who holds
The scepter of heaven and hurls the lightning bolts.
Do not run from me!"
                            She was already running
And had left Lerna's fields behind and the woods
Of Lyrcea, when the god covered the wide earth
In a blanket of mist and stole her chastity.

Juno, meanwhile, looked straight down at Argos
And wondered why this sudden fog had made night   640
Out of brilliant day. She knew there had not been
Any mist from a river or from any damp ground.
She looked around for her husband, suspecting
The intrigue of a spouse so often caught in the act.
When she could not find him anywhere in the skies,
She said, "Either I'm wrong or I'm being wronged."
And she glided down from the top of heaven,
Stood upon the earth and dissolved the clouds.
But Jove had a presentiment of his wife's approach
And had changed the daughter of Inachus   650

Into a glossy heifer. She was still stunning,
Even as a cow. Juno looked at her and couldn't help
But admire her looks. Then she asked whose she was,
Where from, of what stock, as if she didn't know.
Her husband, to forestall further inquiries, maintained
That she was born of the earth, but Juno countered
By demanding her as a gift. What should he do?
Cruel to surrender his love, but suspect not to.
Shame persuaded, Love dissuaded, and Shame
Would surely have yielded to Love, but to refuse   660
So slight a gift as a cow to his sister and wife
Might make the cow seem to be no cow at all.

So Juno received her bovine rival but was still
Suspicious of her husband and more escapades
Until she enlisted Argus, son of Arestor,
To watch over the heifer. Argus' head was ringed
With a hundred eyes that took turns sleeping
Two at a time while the others stood watch,
So whatever way he stood his eyes were on Io,
Even when she was behind his back. In the daytime   670
He let her graze, but when the sun went down
He locked her up with a collar—the indignity!—
Around her neck. Her diet was leaves from trees
And bitter herbs, and instead of a bed the poor creature
Lay on the ground, which was not always grassy,
And she drank from muddy streams. When she would stretch
Her suppliant arms to Argus, she had no arms to stretch,
And when she tried to complain she only mooed.
The sound startled her, and her own voice
Became a new source of fear. She came to the banks   680
Of the Inachus, where she had often played,
But when she saw those strange horns reflected
In the water, she shied away from herself in terror.
The Naiads did not know who she was; Inachus himself
Did not know. But she followed her father,
Followed her sisters, allowed herself to be petted,
Offered herself to be admired. Old Inachus

Held out to her some grass he had plucked. She licked
His hand, but as she kissed her father's palms
She could not hold back her tears. If only she could speak,   690
She would ask for help, tell her name, tell her sad story.
Words wouldn't come, but she managed to paw in the dust
Letters that spelled out her transfiguration.

"What misery," exclaimed her father Inachus,
And draping himself on the lowing heifer's horns
And snow-white neck, he lamented again.

"What misery! Are you really my daughter
Whom I have searched for all over the earth?
Unfound you were a lesser grief than regained.
You are silent and do not respond to my words;   700
You only heave deep sighs from your chest, and—
All you can do—bellow and moo in reply!
Not knowing any better, I was preparing
Marriage rites for you, hoping for a son-in-law
And grandchildren later. But now your husband
Must come from the herd, from the herd a child.
And I cannot even end my sorrows with death.
It hurts to be a god, for death's door is shut,
And my grief extends into eternity."

As he mourned in this way, star-studded Argus   710
Pulled him away, and drove the daughter, torn
From her father's side, into a distant pasture,
Positioning himself on the top of a mountain
From which he could keep watch in all directions.

But heaven's ruler could no longer endure
Io's great suffering. He calls his son
Whom the shining Pleiad bore and orders him
To deliver Argus to death. It does not take long
For Mercury to lace up his winged sandals,
Grab his somniferous wand and put on his cap.   720
His gear in order, the son of Jupiter

Makes the jump from heaven to earth, where
He takes off his cap and sets aside his wings,
Keeping only his wand, which he used like a shepherd
To drive a flock of goats (rustled en route)
Through the back country, playing a pipe as he went.
Juno's guard was captivated by the strange music,
And called out,
                      "You there, whoever you are, you
Might as well sit down here on this rock next to me,
There's no richer grass for grazing anywhere,   730
And you see there's shade here fit for a shepherd."

So Atlas' grandson sat down and passed the day
Talking about this and that and playing his reed pipe,
Trying to overcome those bright, vigilant eyes.
But Argus fought hard against the languors of sleep,
And though he allowed some of his eyes to slumber,
He kept some awake. And since the reed pipe, or syrinx,
Was a new invention, he asked where it came from.

Pan and Syrinx

So the god began:
                      "In Arcadia's cold mountains
There was among the wood nymphs of Nonacris   740
An admired naiad. Her sister nymphs called her Syrinx.
She had eluded the pursuit of more than one satyr
And various other deities of the shadowy woods
And wild countryside. She cultivated the virginity
Of the Ortygian goddess, and in Diana's dress
She could pass for Leto's daughter, except that her bow
Was made of horn and Diana's was gold.
Even so she was often mistaken for the goddess.
Once, she was returning from Mount Lycaeum
When Pan saw her. Crowned with a circlet   750
Of sharp pine needles he called out to her . . ."

Here Mercury stopped with much still to tell—
How the nymph rejected Pan's advances

And fled through the trackless woods until
She came to the quiet, sandy stream of Ladon;
And how, with the water in her path, she prayed
To her aquatic sisters for transfiguration;
How just when Pan thought he had Syrinx in his hands,
Instead of the nymph's body he held marshy reeds,
And how his breath sighing over one reed   760
Made a thin, plaintive sound. The god was taken
With the strange sweetness of the tone, and he said,
"This communion with you I will always have, Syrinx."
And so graduated reeds joined together with wax
Became the instrument that still bears the girl's name.

Io (*continued*)

Mercury was poised to tell the whole story
When he saw that all of the eyes had closed.
He stopped speaking and deepened Argus' slumber
By waving his wand over those languid orbs.
And then he brought his sickled sword down   770
On that nodding head where it joined the neck
And sent it spattering down the steep rocks.
Now you lie low, Argus, and all your lights are out,
Those hundred eyes mastered by one dark night.

Juno took the eyes and set them in the feathers
Of her own bird, filling the tail of the peacock
With starlike jewels. But her anger flared,
And the goddess lost no time in fulfilling it,
Setting a terrifying Fury before the eyes and mind
Of her Argive rival, and planting deep in her breast   780
A blind, compulsive fear that drove her in flight
Across the whole world. In the end it was you,
O Nile, who brought her immense ordeal to a close.
When she reached your waters she fell to her knees
On the riverbank, and turning back her long neck
She lifted her face, which was all she could lift,
To the stars. With groans and tears and pathetic lowing
She seemed to reproach Jupiter, to beg him for an end

To all her sorrows. And Jupiter threw his arms
Around his wife's neck and begged her to end   790
Her vendetta at last, saying, "Put aside your fear.
In the future this girl will never cause you grief."
And he called as witness the waters of Styx.

As the goddess calms down, Io regains
Her previous form and becomes what she was.
The bristles recede, the horns decrease, the great eyes
Grow smaller, the jaws contract, arms and hands
Return, and each solid hoof becomes five nails again.
Only the heifer's milk-white color remains.
Happy to have her two legs back, Io stands   800
Erect now, and fearing her speech will come out as moos,
She cautiously pronounces her neglected words.

Phaëthon and Clymene

Now she is worshipped as a goddess by throngs
Of linen-robed devotees. In due time she bore a child,
Epaphus, believed to be great Jupiter' son,
Coresident of his mother's civic temples.
He had a friend well-matched in age and spirit,
Phaëthon, a child of the Sun, who once began boasting
Of his solar parentage and would not back down
When Inachus' grandson rejected his claim: 810
"You're crazy to believe all that your mother says,
And you're swellheaded about your imagined father."
Phaëthon turned red. He repressed his anger out of shame
But brought Epaphus' slander to his mother Clymene:

"And to make it worse, mother, I, the free, the fierce,
Said nothing. I am ashamed that such a reproach
Has gone unanswered. But if I really am born
Of divine stock, give me some kind of proof,
A claim to heaven."

                      With that he threw his arms
Around his mother's neck and begged her by his own life,   820

Her husband Merops' life, and his sister's marriages
To give him some sign of his true parentage.

Clymene, moved perhaps by her son's entreaties,
Or, more likely, by anger at the charge against her,
Stretched her arms to the sky and, looking up at the sun,
Said,
        "By the glittering radiance that you see here,
My son, and that hears and sees us, I swear
That you were born of this light that rules the world
And are a child of the Sun. If I am lying,
May he never let me look upon him again,   830
And may this be the last light that reaches my eyes!
It would not take long for you to find your father's house.
The country he rises from borders our own.
If you have a mind to do so, go ask the Sun himself!"

Phaëthon beamed happily at his mother's words
And, imagining the heavens in his mind,
He left Ethiopia in a flash, crossed India
Beneath its stars, and reached his father's Orient.

Book 2

Phaëthon and Phoebus

The palace of the Sun soared high on its columns,
Bright with the glint of gold and fiery bronze.
The gables were capped with gleaming ivory,
And the double doors were radiant with silver.
The workmanship surpassed the material,
For Vulcan had carved there the seas that surround
The central lands, the disk of earth, and the sky
That overarches all. The sea held dark blue gods,
Triton blowing his horn, shape-shifting Proteus,
And Aegaeon, each arm around a huge whale;   10
Doris and her daughters were there, some swimming,
Some sitting on a rock to dry their sea-green hair,
Some riding dolphins. While they were not identical,
They bore the resemblance that sisters should share.
The land has men and cities, woods and beasts,
Rivers, nymphs, and other rural deities.
Above these scenes was the shining sky, six signs
Of the zodiac on the right door, and six on the left.

When Clymene's son had climbed the steep path
And come under the roof of his putative father,   20
He turned to move toward him, but stopped in his tracks,
Unable to bear the brightness at closer range.
Robed in purple, Phoebus sat on a throne
Brilliant with emeralds. To his right and left stood
Day and Month and Year and Century,
And the seasons stationed at equal intervals.
Young Spring was there wearing a crown of flowers;
Summer stood there nude, with a garland of grain;
Autumn was stained with the juice of trodden grapes;
And icy Winter bristled with hair white as snow.   30

Seated in the middle, the Sun turned his eyes,
Eyes that see all, at the youth, who stood stunned
By this strange new world, and said to him:

"Why have you come to this high palace, Phaëthon,
A son whom no father should ever deny?"

And Phaëthon replied,
                    "O Universal Light of the World
Phoebus, my father, if I may call you father,
And if Clymene is not disguising her shame—
Give me a token by which all may know me
As your true son, and remove my mind's doubt."   40

He spoke, and his father took off his crown
Of glittering light and had the boy come close.
Embracing him, he said,
                    "You are worthy
To be called my own, and Clymene did tell you
Your true origin. And so you will doubt less,
Whatever you ask of me I will grant to you.
I take as my witness the Stygian marsh
By which the gods swear, though my eyes have not seen it."

His words were no sooner out than the boy asked
To drive his father's chariot for a day   50
And take control of all of that horsepower.
The father regretted his oath. Three times,
Four times, he shook his luminous head, saying,

"Your words show that my own were rash. I wish
That I could take back my promise. I confess,
This alone I would refuse you, my son, but now
All I can do is talk some sense into you.
What you want is not safe, quite beyond your strength
And your boyish years. Your lot is mortal;
What you ask for is not. Unaware,   60
You aspire to more than other gods can handle.

Though each of them may do as he pleases,
None, except myself, has the power to stand
On the running board of the chariot of fire.
Even the Olympian, for all his awesome thunderbolts,
Cannot drive these horses. And who is greater than Jove?
The first part of the road is steep, and my horses,
Though fresh in the morning, struggle to climb it.
In mid-heaven it is impossibly high. I often tremble
To look down from there on the sea and the land,   70
And my heart pounds with fear. The final stage
Is a precipitous drop that needs a firm hand.
Even Tethys, who receives me in waters below,
Fears I will plunge in headfirst. Then too, the sky's dome
Spins around in perpetual motion, drawing along
The high stars with dizzying speed. I make my way
Against this orbital motion, going in opposition
To all else in the universe. Imagine yourself
Driving my chariot. Do you think you could buck
That whirling axis and not be swept away?   80
And perhaps you suppose there are groves up there,
Cities of gods, temples rich with gifts. No,
The road runs through wild, threatening figures,
And even if you stay on course, you still must dodge
The horns of Taurus, the bow of Sagittarius,
Leo's ravenous maw, Scorpio's clutching claws,
And the pincers of Cancer. And the horses themselves,
Breathing fire through their nostrils and mouths,
Are not easy to control. They barely obey me
When their spirits are hot and their necks fight the reins.   90
But you, my son, don't let me give you a fatal gift,
And while there is still time, alter your request.
If you really want assurance that you are my son,
My anxiety should be all the assurance you need;
I am proved your father by a father's fear.
Just look at my face! If only you could look
Into my heart as well, and comprehend
What a father feels inside! Finally, look around
At everything the rich world holds, and choose

From all the boundless goods of earth, sea, and sky   100
Whatever you like. You will be denied nothing.
But this one thing I beg you not to ask, a thing which,
If called by its right name, is not a blessing
But a curse. You are asking for a curse, Phaëthon.
Why are your arms around my neck, foolish boy?
Don't worry, whatever you choose you will get—
I have sworn by the Styx—but choose more wisely!"

The admonition was over, but Phaëthon
Kept fighting back. He pressed on with his plan,
Burning with desire for that chariot.   110
His father delayed as long as he could,
And then led the boy to the sublime vehicle,
The work of Vulcan. Its axle was gold,
As was the chariot pole; the rims of the wheels
Were gold, and the spokes silver. Along the yoke
Chrysolites and gemstones set in a row
Reflected the brilliance of Phoebus' own light.

While the brave young soul gazed in wonder
At this work of art, Aurora awoke and threw open
The glowing doors to her rosy eastern courts.   120
The Morning Star ushered out all the others
And was last to leave his place in the sky.
When the Sun saw him go, saw the skies redden
And the horns of the waning crescent moon vanish,
He ordered the swift Hours to hitch up his horses.
The goddesses, quick to comply, led the stallions,
Breathing fire and sated with ambrosia,
Out from the high stables. Their bridles jingled
While the father anointed his dear son's face
With a sacred unguent to protect it from fire   130
And placed the rays on his head. Foreseeing grief,
And drawing up sighs from his troubled heart, he said:

"If you can take at least some of a parent's advice,
Spare the whip, boy, and pull hard on the reins.

They run fast on their own; your job is to hold back
A spirited team. And don't just go where you please
Driving straight across the five zones of heaven.
The course is laid out on an oblique curve, confined
To the three central zones, avoiding the south pole
And the starlit Bear with her frigid north winds.   140
That is your road—you will see the tracks of my wheels.
And so heaven and earth will receive equal heat,
Do not drive too low or stampede the horses
Up into the aether! Too high will scorch heaven's roof,
Too low the earth. The middle course is safest for you.
Don't veer right toward the writhing Serpent
Or steer left where the Altar lies on the horizon.
Stay between the two. I entrust the rest to Fortune.
I pray that she helps you and guides you better
Than you do yourself.

              While I've been speaking,   150
Dewy Night has touched down on the western shore.
We are summoned, and may delay no longer.
Shining Aurora has put the shadows to flight.
Take the reins, or if your mind can still be changed,
Take my counsel instead of my chariot,
While you can, while you are still on solid ground
And have not yet taken your stand in the car
That you so foolishly want. Let me shed daylight
Over the world, light that you may see without risk."

But Phaëthon is already standing tall   160
In the sleek chariot, and, delirious with joy
To be holding the reins, thanks his father for the gift.

And now Pyrois, Eous, and Aethon,
The Sun's swift horses, and the fourth, Phlegon,
Fill the air with fire as they stamp and whinny
And punish the paddock bars with their hooves.
Tethys, ignorant of her grandson's fates, pushed back
The bars and opened the gates to the infinite skies,
And the horses were off, hooves pounding the air.

They parted the clouds in their path, and, lifted   170
On their wings, they outstripped the East Wind,
Which has its rising in this same quarter.
But the weight was too light for these solar horses,
And the yoke was without its accustomed drag.
As curved ships without the right ballast
Roll off kilter, prone to capsize in open water
Due to their lightness, so too the chariot
Without its usual burden was tossed around
And bounced in the air as if it had no one onboard.
As soon as they felt it, the team ran wild,   180
Leaving the well-worn track and going off course.
The driver panicked. He had no idea
How to handle the reins entrusted to him
Or where the road was. And even if he had known
He wouldn't have been able to master the horses.
Then for the first time the cold Bears grew hot
With the rays of the sun, and tried in vain to plunge
Into the forbidden sea. And Draco, the serpent
Coiled around the icy pole, until then always sluggish
With the arctic chill and formidable to none,   190
Began to seethe and rage with the feverish heat.
They say that you too, Boötes, ran in terror,
Slow though you were and held back by your cart.

When the very unhappy Phaëthon looked down
From heaven's summit and saw the lands
Spread out beneath him far, far below, the blood
Drained from his face, his knees shook in fear,
And his eyes swam with shadows, stunned by the glare.
He wishes now he'd never touched his father's horses
Or succeeded in his quest to know his origin.   200
He would much rather now be called Merops' son
As he is driven like a ship in a northern gale,
A ship whose pilot has dropped the rudder
And abandoned her to the will of the gods.
What should he do? Much of the sky was behind him,
But more was ahead. He measured both in his mind,

Looking toward the west he was not destined to reach,
And then back to the east. Dazed, he has no idea
Of what he should do, and can neither loosen the reins
Nor manage to hold them, nor call the horses by name.   210
And he saw in horror surreal images
Of astral predators strewn through the sky.
There is a place where Scorpio arcs its pincers
And with its hooked tail and curving arms sprawls
Over two constellations. When the boy saw it,
Oozing black venom and threatening to wound him
With its barbed stinger, his mind froze with fear
And he dropped the reins. When the horses felt them
Draped over their backs, they veered off course,
And with nothing to stop them they galloped across   220
Unknown regions of heaven. Rushing wherever
Their momentum took them, they made incursions
Into the fixed stars, hurtling the chariot
Along uncharted tracks, climbing at times
To the high stratosphere and then plunging down
To airspace not much above ground level.
The Moon was amazed to see her brother's horses
Lower than her own.

                       The heated clouds began to smoke,
And the earth burst into flames, the highest parts first,
As deep fissures open and its moisture dries up.   230
Meadows are drifted over with ash, leafy trees burn,
Scorched grain provides its own fuel for fire.
But I bewail lesser things. Walled cities perish,
Entire nations and whole populations
Are reduced to ashes. Woodlands burn with the hills.
Mount Athos is ablaze, Cilician Taurus,
Tmolus and Oeta, Ida, now arid though once
Crowded with springs, maiden Helicon,
And Haemus (not yet with its Oeagrian epithet).
Etna now burns with immense double flames,   240
The twin peaks of Parnassus, Eryx, Cynthus,
Othrys, Rhodope, at last losing its snow,
Mimas, Dindyma, Mycale, and Cithaeron,

Old in religion. Scythia's cold climate offers
Little refuge. The Caucasus is burning,
Ossa, Pindus, and, greater than both, Olympus,
The high Alps, and the cloud-capped Apennines.

Phaëthon sees the whole world on fire.
He cannot bear the terrible heat. The air he sucks in
Feels like it comes from the depths of a furnace,   250
And the chariot glows white-hot. The ashes
And sparks are unendurable; he is enveloped
In a dense pall of smoke, and in that pitchy blackness
He doesn't know where he is or where he is going,
Swept along by the will of the winged horses.

They think it was then that the Ethiopians,
As the heat drew the blood up close to the skin,
Became dark-complexioned. Robbed of their moisture,
Libya's hills then were bleached into desert.
Water nymphs tore their hair and wailed lamentations   260
For their pools and lakes. Boeotia searched
For the waters of Dirce, Argos for Amymone,
Ephyre for Pirene's rills. Nor were the rivers safe
Between their wide banks. The Don turned to steam,
As did old Peneos, Teuthrantean Caïcus,
The swift Ismenus, Arcadian Erymanthus,
The Xanthos (destined to burn yet again),
Tawny Lycormas, the Maeander as it played
In its meandering curves, Mygdonian Melas
And the Taenarian Eurotas. They all burned,   270
Along with the Babylonian Euphrates,
The Orontes, the Thermodon, the rushing Ganges.
The Alpheus boiled, Spercheios' banks burned,
The gold swept along in the Tagus' current
Liquefied in the heat, and the swans that carpeted
Maeonia with song were scorched in the Caÿster.
The Nile fled in terror to the end of the world
And hid its still hidden head, its seven mouths
Dry and empty, seven barren, waterless channels.

The rivers in Thrace, the Hebrus and Strymon,   280
Were likewise parched, as were those in the west,
The Rhine, Rhone, and Po, and the River Tiber,
Whose eddies held promise of universal power.

The ground cracks open, and light streams through the fissures
Down to Tartarus, alarming the underworld king and his queen.
The sea contracts, and what was once wide open water
Is now an ocean of sand; undersea mountains emerge,
Archipelagos added to the scattered Cyclades.
Fish dive deep, and dolphins no longer dare
To arc through the air. The lifeless bodies of seals   290
Float faceup on the sea, and Nereus himself,
The story goes, along with Doris and her daughters,
Hid in warm sea caverns. Three times Neptune tried
To lift his fierce face and arms above the sea's surface
And three times could not bear the incandescent heat.

Though surrounded as she was by a shrinking sea,
With her own streams withdrawn into the darkness
Of her own womb, Mother Earth still lifted up
Her parched and smothered face, and placing a hand
Before her fevered brow, heaved with mighty tremors   300
That shook the world. Then, sinking back a little lower
Than she was before, she spoke in solemn tones:

"If this is your pleasure and I have deserved it,
Why, lord of the gods, is your lightning idle?
If I must perish by fire at least let it be yours
And lighten my loss by having it come from you.
I can hardly open my mouth to speak these words."
The smoke was suffocating her. "See my scorched hair,
The ashes in my eyes and all over my face.
Is this how you reward my fertility, my service   310
In bearing the wounds of plow and mattock,
Worked and worked over year in and year out?
Is it for this that I provide fodder for flocks,

Grain for humankind, and incense for your altars?
But, supposing that I deserve destruction,
What does the sea, or your brother, deserve?
Why are the waters—which are his share by lot—
Reduced to shallows and so much farther from the sky?
But if you could care less about me or your brother,
Pity your own heavens! Look around: 320
The entire vault of heaven is smoking. If the fire
Weakens its structure, your mansions will be ruins.
Even Atlas is struggling and can barely support
The white-hot dome on his shoulders. If the sea,
The land, and the celestial realms perish,
We will all be reduced to primordial chaos!
Save from the flames whatever still survives
And take counsel for the whole of the universe."

Earth stopped speaking, for she could no longer bear
The seething heat, and withdrew into herself   330
And to caverns closer to the realm of shades.
But the Father Almighty called the gods to witness
(And especially the one who had given the chariot)
That unless he came to the rescue, the entire world
Was doomed. He then ascended to heaven's zenith,
His accustomed station when he covers earth with clouds,
Rolls out thunder, and hurls quivering lightning.
But now he has no clouds to cover the earth
Or rain to send down. He does have thunder, though,
And in his right hand balances a lightning bolt   340
Level with his ear, and hurls it at the charioteer,
Jolting him from the car and from his soul as well,
And quenching fire with caustic fire. The horses
Went mad and leapt in different directions,
Wrenching their necks from the yoke and breaking
Free of the bridles. The reins lie here, the axle
Over there, torn from the pole. The wheels
Are shattered, the spokes strewn all over the place
In the shower of debris from the chariot wreck.

But Phaëthon's red hair was a plume of flame   350
As he was propelled in a long arc through the air,
Leaving a trail the way a star sometimes does
When it seems to have fallen from a cloudless sky.
He was received in a distant part of the globe,
Far from his native land, by the greatest of rivers,
The Eridanus, who bathed his steaming face.
The Hesperian Naiads buried his body,
Still smoking from that jagged lightning bolt
And inscribed this epitaph upon the tomb:

HERE LIES PHAËTHON, WHO TOOK HIS FATHER'S REINS.   360
    IF HE LOST HIS HOLD, HIS HIGH DARING REMAINS.

The father, sick with grief, hid his face,
And, if we are to believe it, an entire day passed
Without the sun. But since the wildfires gave light,
The catastrophe served some useful purpose.

Clymene said the words that must be said
In times so terrible, and then, out of her mind
With grief, clawing her breast, she wandered the world,
Looking first for his body, and then his bones,
And at last found his bones buried by the shore   370
Of a distant river. There she sank to her knees
And poured forth tears on the name carved in marble
And caressed it with her open bosom. Her daughters,
The Heliades lamented no less, giving tears
And other useless tribute to the dead, bruising
Their breasts with their palms, calling pitifully
Day and night on Phaëthon, who would never hear them,
And prostrating themselves on his sepulcher.

Four times the Moon had joined her crescent horns
To fill her orb, and, as had become their custom now,   380
The sisters were still mourning, when Phaëthousa,
The oldest, complained as she tried to prostrate herself
That her feet were growing stiff; and when Lampetië,

A radiant nymph, was coming to her aid,
She was rooted to the spot. A third sister, tearing
Her hair with her fingers, held a handful of leaves;
One grieved that her legs were now sheathed in wood,
Another that her arms forked into branches and twigs.
As they wondered at this, bark began to enclose
Their thighs, creep up over their waists, their breasts,   390
Their shoulders, their hands, until all that was left
Were their mouths, calling out for their mother.
But what could Mother do except flit from this one
To that one, kissing their lips as long as she could?
It won't do. She tries to pull the bark from their bodies,
Snapping their twigs in two, but blood trickles out
From each wounded branch. "Please, Mother, stop!"
Cries out whichever is hurt. "Please stop. It is my body
Inside the tree that you're tearing. And now, farewell."
And the bark sealed off her very last words.   400
Tears flow from those trees, and hardened by the sun,
Drip down from the virgin branches as amber,
And the bright river takes them and bears them along
To be worn one day by the brides of Rome.

Cygnus, son of Sthenelus, witnessed this wonder.
Though he was your kin, Phaëthon, on his mother's side,
He was even closer in spirit. Leaving his kingdom
(He ruled Liguria's great cities) he wandered in tears
Along the Eridanus. As he filled its green banks
And woods with grief, and the new stand of poplars   410
Weeping amber tears, his voice grew thin, and feathers
Of white down grew in place of his hair, his neck
Now stretched in an arc out from his chest, a web
Joined his reddening fingers, wings covered his sides
And a blunt beak his mouth. In this way Cygnus
Became a strange, new bird, but did not entrust himself
To the upper air or to Jove, ever mindful
Of the fire that unjustly came from on high.
He sought still pools and placid lakes, making his home
In water, the element opposed to hateful fire.   420

Meanwhile, Phaëthon's father mourns, bereft
Of his bright glory, as if he were in eclipse.
He hates the light, hates himself, hates the day.
He gives his soul over to grief, to grief adds rage,
And refuses his duty to the world.

                          "Enough," he says,
"From the beginning of time it has been my lot
Never to rest. I am weary of my endless toil,
My unhonored labor. Let someone else drive
The chariot of light. If there is no one else,
If all the gods admit it is beyond their power,   430
Let Jove himself do it, so that at least while he tries
To handle my reins he might put down the bolts
That deprive fathers of sons. Then he will know,
When he has felt the strength of those fire-shod horses,
That not to control them does not merit death."

As the Sun speaks, all the gods stand around him,
Pleading with him not to abandon the cosmos
To perpetual shade. Jupiter himself
Fashions excuses for the lightning discharge,
And adds to his prayers a few royal threats.   440
Phoebus finally yokes his horses again,
Trembling still and half-wild with fear, and in his grief
Savages them with goad and lash, savages them
And reproaches them with the death of his son.

Callisto

But the Father Almighty makes a circuit around
Heaven's monumental walls, inspecting them
For any structural faults caused by the fire.
When he sees that they are sound, just as strong
As they should be, he turns his attention
To the earth, and to human affairs.

                           Arcadia   450
Is of particular interest. He sets about restoring
Its springs and rivers, which had not yet
Dared to flow again; he gives the soil grass, leaves

To the trees, and bids the shattered woods grow green.
As he came and went, he would often stop short
At the sight of a girl from Nonacris, passion
Heating up in the marrow of his bones.
She was not the sort of girl to spin soft wool
Or worry about her hair. A simple clasp
Fastened her tunic, and a white headband   460
Held back her loose curls. She sometimes carried
A light javelin in her hand, sometimes a bow,
One of Diana's recruits, and no nymph on Maenalus
Was dearer to her; but no favor lasts forever.

The sun was high, just past the meridian,
When she entered a virgin grove. She slipped
Her quiver from her shoulder, unstrung her bow,
And lay down on the tufted grass, her head
Propped up on her painted quiver. When Jupiter
Saw her there, so worn out and all alone,   470
He said to himself, "My wife will never discover
This little deception, or if she does find out,
It will be well worth the quarrel!" Instantly
He adopted the face and dress of Diana
And said, "Chaste nymph, best of my companions,
What ridges did you hunt today?" She rose
From the turf and replied, "Hail, goddess, greater
Than Jove in my opinion, though he himself
Should hear me say it." He smiled to hear it,
Amused to be preferred to himself, and kissed her,   480
No modest kiss, nor one a virgin would give.
When she started to talk about which woods to hunt,
He stopped her with an embrace, betraying himself
With a less than innocent act. She did struggle,
As much as a woman can—had you seen it,
Juno, you would have been kinder—but what man
Can a girl overcome, and who can overcome Jove?
The god returned to the sky, flush with victory.
The girl loathed the woodlands that knew her secret.
As she retraced her steps she almost forgot   490

To retrieve the quiver and the bow she'd hung up.
But look—here comes Diana with a troop of nymphs
Along Maenalus' ridges, proud of her kills,
And catches sight of the girl and calls to her. At first
She runs, afraid that Jove lurks in Diana's skin,
But when she sees the other nymphs at her side,
She senses no tricks and joins their number. Ah,
How hard not to betray her guilt with her face!
She scarcely lifts her eyes from the ground, nor
Is she found at the goddess' side, at the front   500
Of the group as before. She walks in silence,
And her blushes betray her injured chastity.
If Diana herself were not a virgin,
She would recognize her guilt by a thousand signs.
They say the nymphs recognized it at once.
                                          Nine times
The moon had swollen from crescent to full,
When the goddess Diana, worn out with hunting
And the heat from Helius her brother, came upon
A cool grove through which a murmuring stream
Flowed gently over smooth sand. Voicing her delight,   510
She dipped her feet into the water, and delighting
In this too, she said, "There are no prying eyes here.
Let's bathe nude in the flowing water."
The Arcadian girl blushed. The rest disrobed;
One tried to stall, but as she hesitated
The tunic was removed and her shame revealed
Along with her body. Terrified, and trying to hide
Her belly with her hands, she heard Diana say,
"Begone from here, and do not pollute our sacred spring."
And the goddess expelled her from her company.   520

The Thunderer's wife had known all about this
For a while now, but held her vengeance in check
Until the time was right. There was no reason now
To wait any longer, for the boy Arcas had been born
To her rival, and this in itself infuriated Juno.
When she turned her enraged attention to this, she said,

"There was nothing else left, adulteress, than for you
To become pregnant and highlight your insult to me
By giving birth, publicizing my Jupiter's disgrace.
You won't get away with it. I'll take away that figure   530
You and my husband liked so much, you little slut."

She caught Callisto by her hair and threw her
Facedown in the dirt, and when the girl stretched out
Her arms in supplication, they began to bristle
With rough black hair, her hands curved into paws
With sharp claws, and her face, once praised by Jove,
Became a broad, ugly grin. And so that she could not
Pray to the god or move him with entreaties,
Her power of speech was taken away, and only
A low, menacing growl would come from her throat.   540
Her old mind remained, though now it remained
In the bear she'd become, and her constant moaning
Testified to her pain. She would lift to heaven's stars
What rough hands she had, and though she could not say it,
She still felt Jupiter's ingratitude. How often,
Afraid to sleep in the woods, she paced in front of
Her old home, trespassing in fields that once had been hers.
How often was she driven over rocky ground
By baying hounds, the huntress afraid of hunters!
Often she hid at the sight of wild animals, forgetting   550
What she herself had become, and though she was a bear
She shuddered when she saw other bears on the mountain,
And even feared wolves, although her father was one.

And now Lycaon's grandson Arcas, who knew
Nothing of his parents, had just turned fifteen.
While he was out hunting, scouting the best spots,
And enmeshing Arcadia's woods with his nets,
He came upon his mother, who stopped in her tracks
At the sight of Arcas. She seemed to recognize him.
He shrank back from the gaze of those unmoving eyes,   560
Afraid without knowing why; and as the bear
Started to advance, panting and eager,

He raised his sharp spear to pierce her breast.
But the Omnipotent stopped him, removing at once
Both of the principals and the crime from the scene.
He whisked the pair up through the void in a whirlwind
And set them in the sky as conjoined constellations.

Juno was engorged with rage when she saw her rival
Twinkling among the stars, and went down into the depths
To see grey Tethys and old Ocean, to whom the gods   570
Often pay reverence, and when they asked her
Why she had come, she began:
                              "You ask me
Why I, the queen of the celestial gods am here?
Another woman has replaced me in heaven.
I am a liar if you don't see, when the sky gets dark,
New constellations set on high to spite me,
In the smallest circle right next to the pole.
Why should anyone scruple to offend Juno now
In fear of my wrath, when my harm only helps?
Oh, how great am I, what vast power I have!   580
I make her an animal and now she's a goddess!
That's how I smite those who trespass against me,
That's how mighty I am! He might as well release her
From her animal form and give her back her old face,
Just as he did for Io of Argos! Why not,
With Juno out of the way, put her in my bed
And make himself Lycaon's son-in-law?
But you, if you are upset with this insult
To your foster child, debar those seven stars
From your blue waters, reject constellations   590
Whose path to heaven was paved by prostitution,
And don't let that whore bathe in your pure sea."

★ ★ ★

Jupiter and Europa

Jupiter called his son Mercury aside
And, without mentioning love as a motive,

"Son," he said, "loyal minister of my decrees,   930
Go quickly now in your usual way and glide
Down to that land that sees your mother's star
In the Pleiades from the eastern quadrant.
Sidon it's called. When you see a royal herd grazing
Off in the mountains, drive it down to the sea."

He had no sooner spoken than the cattle were headed
To the designated shore, where a great king's daughter
Used to play in the company of young Tyrian girls.
Majesty and Love do not go well together,
So setting his massive scepter aside,   940
The Gods' Father and Ruler, whose right hand wields
The forked lightning, who shakes the globe with a nod,
Assumed a bull's form and lowed with the cattle,
A beautiful beast shambling through tender grass.
He was as white as pristine, untrodden snow
Before it turns to slush in the South Wind's rain.
His neck rippled with muscles, dewlaps hung in front,
His horns were twisted, but you would have argued
They were made by hand, more lustrous than pearls.
He had no glowering brow or eye full of menace: 950
His expression was calm. Agenor's daughter
Admired him, so beautiful, so unthreatening.
Gentle as he was she feared at first to touch him,
But soon she drew near and held flowers out
To his shining mouth. The lover in him exulted
And while he waited for his expected pleasure,
He kissed her hands, scarcely able to distinguish
Now from soon. At one moment he cavorts
And leaps in the grass, at another he lies down,
Resting his snowy flanks on the yellow sand.   960
As her fear diminishes he offers, first, his chest
For her virgin hands to pat, and then his horns
To be twined with fresh flowers. The princess even
Dares to sit on the back of the bull, unaware
Of whose back it is, while the god moves insensibly
From dry land to shore, testing the shallows
With his deceitful hooves. Then he slips farther out

And soon bears his prize across the high sea.
In terror she watches the shoreline recede,
One hand gripping a horn, the other his back,   970
Her clothes fluttering in a stiffening breeze.

Book 3

Cadmus and the Earthborn People

The god shed his bull disguise, revealed to Europa
His true identity, and reached the island of Crete.
Meanwhile, the girl's father tells his son Cadmus
To go find his stolen sister, threatening him with exile
For failure, and so manages to be devoted
And execrable at once. After roaming the world
To no effect (who could ferret out Jove's loves?),
Agenor's son, now an exile, shuns his fatherland
And his father's wrath and consults the oracle
Of Phoebus Apollo to discover which land   10
He should settle in. This was Phoebus' response:

"A heifer will meet you in an empty field,
One who has never been yoked or drawn a plow.
Follow her wherever she goes, and when she
Lies down in the grass, build your city's walls.
And you shall call the land Boeotia."

Cadmus had no sooner left the Castalian cave,
When he saw a heifer moving slowly along,
Unguarded, and no mark of a yoke on her neck.
He followed her footsteps, and as he walked   20
Silently thanked Apollo for showing the way.
He had just crossed the Cephisus and Panope's fields
When the heifer halted, and lifting to heaven
Her beautiful head with its spiraling horns
She made the air pulse with her lowing. Then,
Looking back at the people following her,
She sank to her knees and lay in the soft grass.
Cadmus gave thanks, kissed this pilgrim land,
And greeted the unknown mountains and plains.

Meaning to sacrifice to Jove he sent out men   30
To find a source of fresh water for libation.
There was an ancient forest nearby, untouched
By any axe, and within it stood a cave
Set in thick shrubs, and with tight-fitting stones
Forming a low arch from which a rich spring flowed.
Hidden in that cave was a serpent, sacred to Mars
And with a magnificent golden crest; his eyes
Flashed fire; his body was swollen with venom;
His triple tongue flickered through three rows of teeth.
When the Tyrian scouting party reached this spring   40
With luckless steps, and their lowered vessel
Made a splashing sound, the dark blue serpent
Thrust his head from the cave with a horrible hiss.
The urns fell from the men's hands, their hearts stopped,
And they couldn't keep their limbs from trembling.
The serpent twists its scaly coils in slithering loops,
Springs himself into a huge arching bow,
And with more than half its length erect in the air
Peers down on the whole forest, his body as large,
If you could take it all in, as the Serpent that lies   50
Outstretched in the sky between the two Bears.
Whether the Phoenicians were preparing for fight
Or flight, or were simply frozen with fear,
We do not know. The serpent attacked instantly,
Killing some with its fangs, others in its coils,
And blasting some with its poisonous breath.

The zenith sun had contracted the shadows.
Cadmus wondered what was keeping his men
And went after them. He wore a lion's skin
And carried a spear with a gleaming iron tip   60
Along with a javelin, and better than any weapon,
He had a brave heart. When he entered the forest
And saw his men's bodies, saw their conqueror
Hulking hugely above them and licking
Their lamentable wounds with his bloody tongue,
"Loyal bodies," he said, "either I avenge your death

Or join you." And he lifted a massive stone
In one hand and put all his weight into the throw.
It would have been enough to make city walls
And their high towers quake, but the serpent escaped   70
Unscathed, protected from that mighty blow
By his armored scales and tough skin beneath.
But that dark, hard skin could not stop the javelin,
Which now stuck in a fold of the serpentine back,
The iron slicing down to the guts. Mad with pain,
He twisted his head toward the wound and bit the shaft
Until he finally worked it loose and tore it out,
But the iron head remained stuck in the spine.
Fresh motivation enhancing his usual rage,
The veins bulge in his throat, and white foam flecks   80
His deadly jaws. His scales rasp against the ground,
And a black breath, as if from the mouth of the Styx,
Fouls the tainted air. He coils in huge spirals,
Rears up straighter than a post, then rushes forward
Like a rain-swollen river, plowing down
All the trees in his path. The son of Agenor
Gives way a little, survives the serpent's attacks
By virtue of the lion's skin and keeps his jaws at bay
With the point of his spear. The serpent is furious,
Snaps uselessly at the iron and clamps it in his teeth.   90
Blood begins to flow from the venomous throat
And stains the green grass, but the wound is slight
Because the serpent keeps drawing back from the thrust,
Protecting his neck and preventing the spear point
From sinking in deeper and being driven home.
But the son of Agenor keeps pushing the iron
Into his throat until at last an oak tree
Blocks the serpent's retreat and his neck is pinned
Against the hardwood. Branches bend under his weight,
And the trunk groans as it is lashed by his tail.   100

As the conquering hero surveys the expanse
Of his conquered foe, a voice makes itself heard,
Impossible to say from where, but a real voice:

"Why, Cadmus, do you gaze at a slain serpent?
You will be gazed at as a serpent yourself."

He stood there a long time, trembling and drained,
The hair on his skin stiff with cold terror,
And then Pallas, helper of heroes, floating down
From the high air, was there, commanding him
To turn the earth and sow the dragon's teeth,   110
And so generate a new people. He obeyed,
And when he had opened a furrow with his plow
He started scattering in the teeth as human seed.
And then, beyond belief, the ground begins to move.
At first the points of spears appear from the furrows,
And then helmets nodding their colored crests;
Soon shoulders and chests come up, and arms
Loaded with weapons, a whole crop of warriors,
Just as when the curtain comes up in a theater
At the end of a festival and its pictures rise,   120
First revealing faces and then gradually the rest
With a steady motion, until whole figures appear
And place their feet on the curtain's lower edge.

Alarmed by this new enemy Cadmus began to arm,
When one of the earthborn people shouted,
"No! Do not get involved in our civil war!"
As his sword came down on one of his brothers
He himself went down with a spear in his back,
But the one who had thrown it lived no longer himself,
Breathing out the air that had just filled his lungs.   130
In the same way the entire mob raged, and they fell
In their war, brothers of a moment killing each other,
Youths with brief lives allotted beating the breast
Of Mother Earth, who grew warm with their blood.
Only five were left, one of whom, Echion,
Dropped his weapons at the command of Pallas
And pledged peace with his surviving brothers.
These men became the Sidonian's companions
When he founded the city foretold by Apollo.

And now Thebes stood, and you could seem, Cadmus,   140
Happy even in exile. The parents of your bride
Were Venus and Mars, and your children were worthy
Of so noble a mother, so many sons and daughters
To remind you of your love, and grandsons too,
Already young men. But a man's last day
Must always be awaited, and no one counted happy
Until he has died and received due burial.

Diana and Actaeon

Your first reason to grieve, Cadmus, amid
So much happiness, was your grandson Actaeon.
Strange horns grew on his forehead, and his hounds   150
Glutted themselves on the blood of their master.
But if you look well you will find the fault was Fortune's,
Not Actaeon's sin. What sin is there in error?

The mountain was stained with the slaughter of beasts,
Noon had already contracted the shadows,
And the sun was midway between both horizons,
When the imperturbable young Boeotian
Spoke to his hunting companions as they wandered
The trackless wild:
                    "Our nets and blades are wet with blood.
The day has brought us enough luck. When Aurora   160
Rolls in another dawn on her saffron wheels
We'll go at it again. But now Phoebus
Is in midcourse and splits the fields with heat.
Call it a day and bring in the nets!"
                                      The men
Did as he said and left off their work.

There was a valley there called Gargaphië,
Dense with pine and bristling cypress, and sacred
To Diana, the high-skirted huntress. Deep in the valley
Is a wooded cave, not artificial but natural,
But Nature in her genius has imitated art,   170
Making an arch out of native pumice and tufa.

On the right a spring of crystal-clear water
Murmured as it widened into a pool
Edged with soft grass. Here the woodland goddess,
Weary from the hunt, would bathe her virgin limbs.
When she arrives there she hands her spear and quiver
And unstrung bow to one of her nymphs. Another
Takes her cloak over her arm, two untie her sandals,
And Crocale, cleverer than these, gathers up
The goddess' hair from her neck and ties it in a knot   180
While her own is still loose. Nephele, Hyale,
Rhanis, Psecas, and Phiale draw water
And pour it from huge urns over their mistress.

While Diana was taking her accustomed bath there,
Cadmus' grandson, his work done for the day,
Came wandering through the unfamiliar woods
With uncertain steps and, as Fate would have it,
Into the grove. As soon as he entered the grotto,
The nymphs, naked as they were and dripping wet,
Beat their breasts at the sight of the man, filled the grove   190
With their sudden shrill cries, and crowded around
Their mistress Diana, trying to hide her body with theirs.
But the goddess stood head and shoulders above them.
Her face, as she stood there, seen without her robes,
Was the color of clouds lit by the setting sun,
Or of rosy dawn. Then, though her nymphs pressed close,
She turned away to one side and cast back her gaze,
And, as much as she wished she had her arrows at hand,
What she had, the water, she scooped up and flung
Into that male face, sprinkling his hair with vengeful drops   200
And adding these words that foretold his doom:
"Now you may tell how you saw me undressed,
If you are able to tell!" With that brief threat
She gave his dripping head the horns of a stag,
Stretched out his neck, elongated his ears,
Exchanged feet for hands, long shanks for arms,
Covered his body with a spotted hide,
And instilled fear in him. Autonoë's heroic son

Took off, marveling at how fast he was running.
But when he saw his face and horns in a pool,   210
He tried to say, "Oh, no," but no words came.
He groaned, the only sound he could make,
And tears ran down cheeks no longer his own.
Only his mind was unchanged. What should he do?
Return home to the palace, or hide in the woods?
Shame blocked one course, and fear the other.

While Actaeon hesitated his dogs spotted him.
First Blackfoot and keen-nosed Tracker bayed,
Tracker a Cretan, a Spartan breed Blackfoot.
Then others rushed at him swifter than wind,   220
Greedy, Gazelle, and Mountaineer, Arcadian all,
Powerful Deer Slayer, Hunter, and Whirlwind.
Then Wings, and Chaser the bloodhound, and Woody,
Lately gored by a boar, and wolf-bred Valley,
Trusty Shepherd and Snatcher with both her pups.
There was lean Catcher, a Sicyonian hound,
Runner and Grinder, Spot and Tigress,
Mighty and Whitey and black-haired Soot.
These were followed by Spart, known for his strength,
And by Stormy and Swift and the speedy Wolf   230
With her brother Cypriot. Next was Grasper,
A white spot in the middle of his jet-black forehead,
Blacky and Shaggy and Fury and Whitetooth,
With a Cretan sire and a Spartan dam,
Bell-toned Barker—and others we need not name.
The whole pack, lusting for prey, gave chase
Over cliffs and crags and inaccessible rocks,
Where the way was hard and where there was no way.
He fled through places where he had often chased,
And it was his own hounds he fled. He longed to shout: 240
"I am Actaeon! Know your master!"
But words wouldn't come, and the sky rang with barking.

Blackhair bit him in the back, then the bitch Killer,
Then Hill got hold of a shoulder and wouldn't let go.

These three had left late but got ahead of the others
By a shortcut over the mountain. While they held
Their master down, the rest of the pack converged
And sank their teeth into him. Soon there was no place
Left on his body to wound. He groans, making a sound
That is not human, but still not one any deer could make,   250
And fills the familiar ridges with his mournful cries.
On his knees now, he turns his silent eyes
From side to side, as if he were a suppliant
Stretching out his arms. And now the ravenous hounds
Are urged on by his friends, who know no better,
With their usual yells, looking around for Actaeon,
And outdoing each other with their shouts, "Actaeon!"
As if their friend were absent. He turns his head
At the sound of his name, but they go on complaining
That he is not there and through his sluggishness   260
Is missing the spectacle their prey presents.
He wishes he were absent, but he is there alright,
And would rather see than feel what his dogs are doing.
They are all over him, their jaws into his flesh,
Tearing apart their master in a deer's deceptive shape.
They say that Diana's anger was not appeased
Until he ended his life as a mass of wounds.

Jupiter and Semele

Opinion is divided: to some the goddess
Was unjustly vindictive for simply being seen;
Others praise her and call her violence worthy   270
Of her severe virginity. Both sides have a case.
Only Jupiter's wife neither praises nor blames
So much as she is glad that the house of Agenor
Has suffered catastrophe. By now the goddess
Had shifted her hatred of Europa to those
Connected to her Tyrian rival by birth.
Then another grievance ousted the old one,
The fact that Semele was pregnant by Jove.
As she warmed up her tongue for her usual reproaches,

It hit her:
                    "What have I ever gained from reproaches?   280
It's her I have to get if I am rightly to be called
Juno most great, if I am to hold the jeweled scepter,
If I am the queen, the wife and sister of Jove—
Well, the sister at least. . . . But then I think she is content
With her little secret, a minor dent in my marriage,
Which would be fine if she were not pregnant!
That is what really damages me—the swollen belly
That makes her crime visible. And that she wants
What I have barely achieved, to be the mother
Of Jupiter's child. She trusts her beauty that much.   290
I'll make that trust betray her. I am not Saturn's daughter
If her precious Jove doesn't plunge her into the Styx."

She rose from her throne and, wrapping herself
In an ochre cloud, she came to Semele's door
And stayed in the cloud until she disguised herself
As an old woman grey in the temples, plowing
Wrinkles into her skin and walking bent over
With faltering steps. Assuming also the voice
Of an old woman, she became Beroë,
Semele's Epidaurian nurse. Gossiping on,   300
Jupiter's name came up, and the disguised goddess sighed,

"I hope he really is Jupiter. I mistrust things like that.
Many men have gone into chaste girls' bedrooms
Under the name of a god. And it's not enough
For him to be Jove. He has to give proof of his love
If it really is him. Ask him to embrace you
In the same form, the same size, as Juno herself
Receives him—and with all the marks of his power."

This is how Juno set up the guileless Semele,
Who asked Jove for a gift yet to be named,   310
To which request the god responded,
                                        "Choose,

And you shall not be refused. Believe me:
I swear by the powers of the churning Styx,
Whose divinity all the gods hold in awe."

And Semele, happy to have prevailed
In what would be her destruction, and doomed
By her lover's compliance, said to him,

"Give yourself to me in just the same form
As you have when you and Juno make love."

The god wanted to stop her in midsentence,   320
But the words were already out. He groaned.
She cannot retract her wish, nor he his oath,
And so in utter gloom he ascends the steep sky.
Lifting an eyebrow he draws in mists and clouds
And brews up a storm with wind and lightning,
Taking up last the inevitable thunderbolts.
As best he could, he reduced his potency,
Choosing not, for instance, the bolts that blasted
Typhoeus from heaven, bolts far too lethal,
But a lighter bolt the Cyclopes had forged,   330
One with less firepower and containing less ire;
Ordnance Number Two the gods all call it.
Taking one of these he entered the palace
Of the son of Agenor. Semele's mortal body,
Unable to endure the celestial explosion,
Was incinerated in the conjugal embrace.
The tender babe, still unformed, was snatched
From his mother's womb, and, if it can be believed,
Sewn into his father's thigh, where he was brought to term.
His mother's sister, Ino, secretly cradled him,   340
And then he was given to the nymphs of Nysa,
Who hid him in their cave and nursed him with milk.

Tiresias

While Fate worked itself out on earth in this way,
And the cradle of twice-born Bacchus was safe,

They say that Jupiter, soused with nectar,
Put aside his grave concerns and joking around
With an idle Juno said to her, "Your sex's pleasure
Is clearly greater than any felt by males."
She said no, and so they agreed to ask Tiresias
His opinion, familiar as he was with either sex.   350
For he had once struck with his staff two great serpents
As they were mating in the greenwood,
And, transformed amazingly from man to woman,
Spent seven autumns in that state. In the eighth
He saw the same two snakes again and said,

"If hitting you has power sufficient
To change the sex of the author of the blow,
I'll strike you again now."
                The vipers being struck,
His former form returned and he was himself again.
Chosen as arbiter of this lighthearted spat,   360
He confirmed Jove's opinion. Saturnian Juno,
Taking it harder than the case warranted,
Condemned the umpire to everlasting blindness.
The Almighty Father could not render null and void
Another god's decree, but in recompense
For his loss of sight, gave Tiresias the power
To see the future, lightening the penalty
With this honor. He went on to be celebrated
Throughout the cities and towns of Boeotia
For the faultless responses he gave to petitioners.   370

Echo and Narcissus

The first to test the truth of his utterances
Was Liriope, a water-blue nymph
Caught by Cephisus in a bend of his river
And prevailed upon by force. When this beauty
Gave birth, it was to a child with whom even then
One could fall in love. She called him Narcissus.
When Tiresias was asked if this boy would live
To a ripe old age, the soothsayer replied,

"If he never knows himself." The seer's words
Long seemed empty, but the outcome—the way he died,   380
The strangeness of his passion—proved them to be true.

Narcissus had just reached his sixteenth birthday
And could be thought of as either a boy or a man.
Many a youth and many a girl desired him,
But in that tender body was a pride so hard
That not a youth, not a girl ever touched him.
Once, when he was driving spooked deer into nets,
He was seen by a nymph who could not stay quiet
When another was speaking, or begin to speak
Until someone else had—resounding Echo.   390

Up until then Echo had a body, not just a voice,
But talkative as she was she could only speak
As she does now, repeating the last words said.
Juno had made her like this because many times
When she might have caught Jove on top of some nymph
Up in the hills, Echo would cleverly detain the goddess
In long conversation until the nymph had fled.
When Saturn's daughter realized this, she said,
"This tongue that has tricked me is hereby restricted
To only the briefest use of speech."

                             The outcome   400
Confirmed her threat, and Echo can only repeat
The final words of whatever she hears. Now,
When she saw Narcissus wandering the countryside
She flushed with love and followed him secretly.
The more she followed him, the hotter she burned
From his proximity, the way sulphur smeared
On the top of a torch ignites when a lit torch
Is brought close to it. Ah, how often she wishes
She could go up to him with seductive words
And whisper prayers in his ear, but her nature   410
Won't let her, or even allow her to initiate talk.
But what it will allow she is prepared for:
To wait for words she might return as her own.

So when the boy, separated by chance
From his loyal companions, cried out, "Anyone here?"
"Here," Echo responded. Narcissus was puzzled.
He looked around in every direction and shouted
"Come!" and "Come!" Echo calls to the caller.
He looks behind, sees no one coming, calls again,
"Why run from me?" and gets his own words back.   420
He stands still, beguiled by the answering voice,
And cries, "Meet me here; I'm here!" And Echo,
Never again to answer a sound more gladly, cries,
"I'm here!" and follows up her words by coming
Out of the woods to throw her arms around
The neck she longed for. He runs, and says on the run,
"Take your hands off! I'll die before I let you have me!"
And Echo comes back with nothing but "Have me!"
Rejected, she lurks in the woods, hiding her shamed face
In the leaves, and lives from then on in lonely caves.   430
Still, love clings to the spurned girl and grows on grief.
Sleepless and anxious, she begins to waste away;
Her skin shrivels and her body dries up, until
Only her voice and bones are left, and then
Only her voice. They say her bones turned into stone.
She hides in the woods, and is seen no more in the hills
But can be heard by all, and lives on as sound.

So Narcissus mocked this girl, as he had mocked
Others before, nymphs of water and mountain,
And the company of men. One of these scorned youths   440
Lifted his hands to the heavens and prayed,
"So may he himself love, and not get what he loves!"
A just prayer, to which Nemesis assented.

There was an unsullied pool with silvery water
That no shepherds used, no pasturing goats
Or any other cattle, and that no bird or beast
Or even falling twig ever caused to ripple.
It was surrounded with grass fed by its moisture
And shaded by trees that kept it from getting too warm.

Narcissus, worn out and hot from hunting,   450
Lies down here, drawn by the setting and the pool,
And, seeking to quench his thirst, finds another thirst,
For while he drinks he sees a beautiful face
And falls in love with a bodiless fantasy
And takes for a body what is no more than a shadow.
Gaping at himself, suspended motionless
In the same expression, he is like a statue
Carved from Parian marble. Prone on the ground
He looks at the double stars that are his eyes,
His hair, worthy of Bacchus, worthy of Apollo,   460
His impubescent cheeks, his ivory neck, the glory
That is his face, the blush mixed with snowy white,
And admires all for which he is himself admired.
He desires himself without knowing it is himself,
Praises himself, and is himself what is praised,
Is sought while he seeks, kindles and burns with love.
How often did he offer ineffective kisses
To the elusive pool? How often plunge his arms
Into the water to clasp the neck he saw there
And fail to take hold of himself? He does not know   470
What he sees, but what he sees he burns for,
And the same illusion lures and lies to his eyes.
Gullible boy, grasping at passing images!
What you seek is nowhere. If you look away
You lose what you love. What you see is a shadow,
A reflected image, and has nothing of its own.
It comes with you and it stays with you,
And it will go with you, if you are able to go.

No thought of food, no thought of rest can draw him
Away from that spot. Sprawled on the shaded grass   480
He gazes at the mendacious vision with eyes
That cannot get enough and through which he perishes.
Lifting himself up a little and stretching his arms
To the surrounding trees, he cries,
                                        "Is there anyone,

O trees, who has ever been more cruelly in love?
You know, for you've been convenient cover
For many couples. Do you remember
In ages past (for your life spans centuries)
Anyone who has ever pined away like this?
I'm in love and I see him, but what I see and love   490
I cannot find. What a deluded lover!
And to make it worse for me, no great ocean
Separates us, no road, no mountain, no shut city gates.
A little water keeps us apart!
                              He wants to be held.
Whenever my lips approach the limpid water,
He tries to come to me with his face upturned.
You'd think he could be touched, so small a thing
Stands in the way of our love.
                              Whoever you are,
Come out! My looks and my age can't be the sort
You would shun. Even nymphs have been in love with me.   500
You give me some cause for hope with your friendly smile,
And when I stretch out my arms, you stretch yours, too.
When I smile, you smile back, and I have often seen
Tears in your eyes when I am in tears. When I nod
You do too, and from the way your lovely lips move
I suspect you answer my words as well, though yours
Never reach my ears.
                              Oh—that's me! I just felt it,
No longer fooled by my image. I'm burning with love
For my very own self, burning with the fire I lit.
What should I do? Beg or be begged? Why beg at all?   510
What I desire I have. Abundance makes me a beggar.
Oh, if only I could withdraw from my body, and—
Strange prayer for a lover—be apart from my beloved.
And now I'm growing weak with grief; not much time
Is left for me, and I will die in the prime of my life.
Death is not heavy for me, but the end of my sorrows.
I wish that my beloved could live longer, but now
We two die with one heart, and in the same breath."

He spoke and, beside himself with grief, turned
To the same face again, but his tears disturbed the pool,   520
And the reflection was lost in the troubled water.
When he saw the image disappearing, he cried,

"Where are you going? Stay! It would be cruel
To desert your lover. Let me at least look at
What I cannot touch, and feed my obsession."

As he grieved, he opened the top of his tunic
And beat his bare breast with his ashen hands.
His chest took on a roseate glow, just as apples
Can be pale in one part and flush red in another,
Or as grapes in a cluster begin to turn purple   530
As they are just getting ripe. When he saw this
In the water, after it had again become clear,
He could bear no more, and as yellow wax melts
Over a gentle flame, or frost in the morning sun,
So too Narcissus, thin and meager with love,
Melts and is consumed by a slow, hidden fire.
No longer is his color a blushing white,
He no longer has his old vigor and power
And all that made him so beautiful to see—
Not at all same body that Echo once loved.   540
When she saw him now, though she was still angry,
She grieved for him, and whenever the poor boy said,
"Alas," her responsive voice repeated, "Alas."
And when his hands beat on his shoulders and arms,
She gave back the sound of his lamentation.
His last words were, as he gazed into the pool,
"Ah, loved in vain, beloved boy," and the place
Rang with these words. And when he said good-bye,
Echo said good-bye too. His weary head drooped
To the green grass, and death closed the eyes   550
That had gazed in wonder at their master's beauty;
And even after he had gone to the world below,
He kept gazing at himself in the waters of Styx.
His naiad sisters beat their breasts, cut their hair

For their brother, and the dryads, too, lamented,
And all the sounds of woe were repeated by Echo.
And now they were preparing the funeral pyre,
Shaking the torches and readying the bier,
But Narcissus' body was nowhere to be found.
In place of his body they found a flower   560
With white leaves surrounding a saffron center.

★ ★ ★

Book 4

★ ★ ★

Pyramus and Thisbe

Pyramus and Thisbe, he the loveliest of boys,
She the most beautiful girl in the Orient,
Lived next door to each other in the steep city
They say Semiramis encircled with walls of brick.
Proximity led to their early acquaintance;
Love grew with time; and they would have married,   70
But their parents forbade it. What they could not forbid
Was the mutual passion they felt for each other.
There was no go-between; their talk was nods and gestures,
And the more the fire was covered, the hotter it burned.
There was a slender chink in the common wall
Between the two houses, from when they were built.
No one had noticed this crack in all these years—
But what does love not see? You lovers discovered it
And made it a channel for speech. Your loving words
Would slip safely through it in the softest whispers.   80
Often, when they had moved into place, Thisbe here,
Pyramus there, and each had felt the other's breath,
They would say,
                    "Jealous wall, why do you stand
Between lovers? Would it be asking too much
For you to let us embrace, or at least open enough
To allow us to kiss? Not that we are ungrateful.
We owe it to you, we admit, that our words
Have passage to the ears that long to hear them."

So they would talk in frustrated separation,
And when night came on they said "Good-bye,"   90
Each pressing their lips on one side of the wall,

Kisses that did not go through to the other side.
The next dawn had banished the stars of night,
The sun's rays had dried the frosty grass,
And the lovers came to their accustomed place.
After many whispered complaints the pair decided
That they would try to slip past their guardians
In the still of night, and when they were outdoors
They would leave the city as well. And they agreed,
So as not to be wandering around in the fields,   100
To meet at Ninus' tomb and hide under its tree.
The tree there was full of snow-white berries,
A tall mulberry tree next to a cool spring.
They liked the plan. The light seemed to last forever,
Then sank into the waters from which night arose.

Stealthily cracking open the door Thisbe sneaks out
Through the shadows with veiled head, comes to the tomb
And sits beneath the appointed tree. Love made her bold.
But now here comes a lioness, her jaws smeared
With the blood of cattle she's just killed, on her way   110
To slake her thirst at the spring. Babylonian Thisbe
Sees her far off by the light of the moon
And runs on trembling feet into a dark cave,
And as she runs her cloak slips off her back.
When the savage lioness has drunk her fill
She turns back to the woods and happens upon
The cloak (without the girl in it) and shreds it
In her bloody jaws. Coming out a little later,
Pyramus sees the tracks the lioness left
In the deep dust. The color drains from his face,   120
And when he finds the cloak too, smeared with blood,

"One night," he cries, "will be the death of two lovers,
But of the two she was more deserving of life,
And mine has done all the harm. I have destroyed you,
Poor girl, telling you to come by night to this place
Full of terror, and not coming first myself!
Come and tear my body apart, devour my flesh,

Gulp down my guilty heart with your savage jaws,
O all of you lions who have lairs in this cliff!
But it is cowardly just to pray for death."   130

He picked up Thisbe's cloak and carried it
To the shade of the trysting-tree. And while
He kissed and shed tears upon the garment
He knew so well, he cried, "Drink my blood too!"
Drawing the sword that hung by his waist,
He drove it down deep into his flank, then, dying,
Withdrew it from the hot wound. As he lay
Stretched out on the earth his blood spurted high,
Just as when a lead pipe has sprung a leak
At a weak spot, and through the hissing fissure   140
Long jets of water shoot far in the air.
The fruit on the tree, sprinkled with Pyramus' blood,
Turned dark; and the tree's roots, soaked with his gore,
Dyed the mulberries the same purple color.

And now Thisbe, still afraid, but anxious too
That her lover will miss her, comes back from the cave,
Seeking Pyramus with her eyes and her soul
And excited to tell him about her brush with death.
She recognizes the place and the shape of the tree,
But the color of the fruit makes her wonder   150
If this is really it. While she hesitates, she sees
A body writhing on the blood-soaked ground.
She stepped back, her face paler than boxwood,
Shivering like the sea when a light breeze
Grazes its surface, but when, a moment later,
She recognized her lover, she slapped her guiltless arms
In loud lamentation and tore her hair out,
And holding his beloved body she filled his wounds
With her tears, mingling them with his blood,
And as she kissed his cold lips, she wailed,   160

"Pyramus, what happened, what took you from me?
Answer me, Pyramus. It's your dearest Thisbe
Calling you. Please listen, please lift up your head."

At Thisbe's name, Pyramus lifted his eyes,
Heavy with death, saw her, and closed them again.
Then she noticed her cloak, and saw his ivory scabbard
Without his sword in it, and said,
                                            "Your own hand,
And your love, killed you, poor boy. I, too, have a hand
Brave for this one deed; I too have love, and it will give me
The strength to face wounds. I will follow you in death,   170
And I will be called the most wretched cause
And companion of your death. Death alone
Could tear you from me, but not even death will.
And I pray to my wretched parents and to his
On behalf of both of us: do not begrudge
A common tomb to those whom faithful love
And death's final hour have joined. And you, O tree,
Whose branches now cover one pitiful body
And soon will cover two, keep our death's tokens
And always have fruit that is dark and mournful   180
As a memorial to the blood that we both shed."

She spoke, and placing the point beneath her breast
She fell onto the blade, still warm with her lover's blood.
Her prayers touched the gods and touched their parents,
For mulberries turn dark red when they ripen,
And the lovers' ashes rest in a single urn.

★ ★ ★

Salmacis and Hermaphroditus

Learn now why the infamous spring of Salmacis
Enervates men who bathe in its waters. The cause
Is hidden, but the font's power well-known.
Mercury and Venus had a little boy
Whom naiads nursed in the caverns of Ida.
You could tell from his face who his parents were,
And he was named after both his mother and father.
When he turned fifteen he left his native mountains
And nourishing Ida. Exploring new places

And seeing unknown rivers was all his joy, 330
His enthusiasm making light of the toil.
He even reached Lycia and neighboring Caria,
And there he saw a pool of crystal water,
Clear to the bottom. There were no marsh reeds,
Barren sedge or rushes, only translucent water
Edged with fresh turf and grass verdant year-round.
A nymph lived in that pool, a nymph not inclined
To hunt or shoot arrows or go racing along,
The only naiad unknown to Diana.
Her sisters were always saying to her, 340
"Salmacis, pick up a javelin or a painted quiver
And vary your leisure with a little hard hunting."
But she did not pick up a javelin or painted quiver
Or vary her leisure with any hard hunting.
She only bathes her beautiful limbs in her pool;
Often arranges her hair with a boxwood comb;
Looks into the water to see what becomes her;
Wraps her body in a transparent robe
And reclines in the leaves or on the soft grass.
She also picked flowers, and was picking flowers 350
When she saw the boy and wanted to have what she saw.

But, eager as she was, she didn't go up to him
Until she composed herself, looked at her robes
From all angles, touched up her face, and did
Everything she could to look beautiful.
Then she said:

    "Boy or god? If you are a god
You must be Cupid. But if you are a mortal
Blessed be your parents, your brother, your sister,
If you have one, and the woman who nursed you.
But happier than any of these is your bride to be, 360
If there is any girl you think worthy. If there is one,
Let me steal my pleasure. If there is no one yet,
Let me be the one, and let's get married right now."

The naiad fell silent. A blush crossed the boy's cheeks,
For he knew nothing of love, but it was a becoming blush,

The color of apples ripening in a sunny orchard,
Of dyed ivory, or the moon's scarlet glow
When bronze cymbals clash to end an eclipse.
When the nymph kept begging for a sister's kiss
At least, and was twining her arms around   370
His ivory neck, he cried out, "Just stop!
Or I'll leave this spot, and leave you with it."
Salmacis trembled and said, "It's all yours,"
And turning away, pretended to leave.
But she kept looking back, and hid in a thicket,
Crouching on one knee. He, as a boy will
Who thinks he's alone, explored the green bank
And dipped first his toes in the ripples, and then
His feet up to the ankles. Finding the water
Enticing, and just the right temperature,   380
He slipped the clothes from his supple body.
The nymph was spellbound, burning with passion,
And her eyes now were as bright as sunlight
Reflected in a mirror. She could barely endure
Any more delay, any further deferral of joy,
And was out of her mind with desire to hold him.
The boy, clapping his body with cupped palms,
Dove in quickly and began swimming the crawl,
His body gleaming in the translucent water
As if it were an ivory figurine, or a lily   390
Encased in glass.
          "I've got him now!" cried the nymph,
As she threw off her clothes and dove into the pool.
He tries to hold her off as she steals contested kisses,
Runs her hands down his body, fondles a reluctant breast,
Enfolds him on one side and then on the other.
Finally, as he struggled to release himself,
She twisted around him as if she were a snake
Snatched by an eagle up into the sky:
Hanging from his claws the snake slithers around
The raptor's head and feet and entangles his wings;   400
Or as if she were ivy entwining a tree trunk;
Or an octopus holding its prey undersea
With its tentacles wrapped completely around it.

The boy hung in there and denied the nymph
The pleasure she hoped for, and yet she held on tight,
As if her whole body were welded on to his,
"You may fight me, you little rascal," she said,
"But you'll never escape. Gods, may the day not dawn
That will separate him from me or me from him!"
Her prayer was answered. Their bodies were blended   410
Into one face and form. Just as when a twig
Is grafted onto a tree, you can see two branches
Mature into one, so too these bodies fused
In tenacious embrace, not two, not double,
Neither woman nor man, and yet somehow both.

When he saw that the waters he entered as a male
Had left him half a man and softened his limbs,
Hermaphroditus stretched out his hands and cried
In a voice no longer manly,
                                        "Father and Mother,
Grant to the son who bears both of your names   420
That whoever enters this pool as a man
Comes out as a half man, weakened by the water."

His parents blessed the words of their biform son
And drugged the pool to engender confusion.

★ ★ ★

Cadmus and Harmonia

[Cadmus and Harmonia had four daughters: Agave, Autonoë, Semele, and
Ino. In a Bacchic frenzy, Agave tore apart her son Pentheus with the aid of
Autonoë and Ino. Autonoë was the mother of Actaeon, whose disastrous
tale is presented earlier in this volume—as is Semele's. Ino, pursued by her
maddened husband, jumped off a cliff with her infant son; the two were
transformed into divinities of the sea.]

Agenor's son Cadmus did not know that his daughter
And little grandson were now sea gods. Overwhelmed

By the string of disasters, the suffering he had seen,
He now left the city he had founded, as if
The place itself and not his own misfortunes
Were weighing upon him. His long wandering
Took him and his wife to Illyria's borders,
Where, sad and old, they thought of their family's   630
Original destiny and rehearsed their sorrows.
Cadmus said,
    "That serpent I pierced with my spear
Must have been sacred. There I was, fresh from Sidon,
And I scattered its teeth, a strange seed, on the earth.
If that is what the gods have been avenging
In their terrible anger, may I lay out my length
As a long-bellied snake."
      And as he spoke, he did
Lay out his length as a long-bellied snake
And felt his skin turn into hard black scales
Checkered with blue. As he lay on his stomach   640
His legs fused together and tapered to a point.
What was left of his arms he stretched out to his wife,
And with tears running down his still human cheeks,

"Come here," he said, "my poor, ill-starred wife,
While there is still something left of me. Come here
And touch me, hold my hand while it is still a hand,
While the serpent has not yet usurped me completely."

He wanted to say much more, but suddenly
His tongue was forked and words wouldn't come,
And even plaintive sounds came out as a hiss,   650
The only voice that his nature allowed him.
Then, striking her naked breast with her hands,
Harmonia cried out,
    "My poor Cadmus, wait!
Shake this off, this monstrosity! Cadmus,
What is it? Where are your feet, your hands,
Your shoulders, your face, your color—everything
Changing as I speak? Change me as well, you gods,

Into this same serpentine form!"
                                        She spoke,
And his tongue flickered over the face of his wife,
And he slid down between the breasts that he loved,   660
And his embrace sought the neck he knew so well.
Their companions were horrified, but Harmonia stroked
The glistening neck of the crested serpent,
And suddenly not one but two snakes were there,
Their coils intertwined, until they sought the shelter
Of the neighboring woods. And even now as serpents
They neither avoid people nor try to harm them,
Quietly remembering what they once were.

Perseus and Andromeda

A great consolation to them in their altered form
Was their grandson, worshipped now in conquered India,   670
And adored as well in Achaean temples.
Only Acrisius, son of Abas, born
Of the same stock as the god, still banned him
From his city, Argos, campaigning against him
And refusing to admit he was Jupiter's son.
Nor would he admit that Perseus, whom Danaë
Had conceived in golden rain, was Jupiter's son.
But truth has its own power, and Acrisius
Soon regretted that he had repulsed the god
And not acknowledged his grandson. The one   680
Had now been installed in heaven; the other
Was soaring through thin air on whistling wings,
Bearing the snake-haired monster's memorable spoils.
As the victor hovered over the Libyan desert
Bloody drops from the Gorgon's head fell down
And were received by Earth, who reanimated them
As various species of snakes, and this is why
The land there swarms with poisonous vipers.

From there he was driven by conflicting winds
Like a raincloud through vast regions of air.   690
He flew over the whole world, looking down

From dizzying heights on distant lands. Three times
He saw the cold stars of the Bears, and thrice
The Crab's claws. He was blown more than once
Beyond the western horizon, and into the east,
And now as the day faded, wary of the night
He put down in the farthest reaches of the west,
In Atlas' kingdom, hoping to catch a few hours sleep
Before the Morning Star summoned Aurora
And Aurora in turn the chariot of Day.
                                    Here Atlas,   700
Son of Iapetus, who for sheer bulk
Exceeded all men, ruled the edge of the world
And the sea that welcomes the Sun's panting horses
And his weary chariot. He had a thousand flocks,
And as many herds of cattle, wandering
Grassy plains that stretched on without borders.
And there was a tree whose golden leaves
Concealed golden branches and apples of gold.

"My lord," Perseus said to him, "if high birth
Carries any weight with you, mine is from Jupiter;   710
Or if you admire great deeds, you'll admire mine.
I ask for hospitality and a place to rest."

But Atlas remembered an ancient prophecy
Given to him by Themis on Mount Parnassus:
"Atlas, a day will come when your tree will be stripped
Of all its gold, and a son of Jupiter will take the credit."
Fearing this, Atlas had enclosed his orchard
With massive walls, and set a huge dragon to guard it,
And he kept all strangers away from his borders.
Now he said to Perseus,
                            "Get out of here,   720
Or your supposed glory and that Jupiter of yours
Will be long gone."
                        His heavy hands backed up
The threat with force. Perseus interspersed
Gentle words into his heroic resistance,

But finding himself outmanned (who could outman
Atlas himself?) he said to him,
                              "Well, now,
Since you are able to show me so little kindness,
Here's a little kindness for you!"
                              And turning away,
He held out on his left the horrible head
Of the Gorgon Medusa. As big as he was,   730
Atlas immediately turned into a mountain
Of just the same size. His hair and beard
Were changed into trees, and into ridges
His shoulders and hands. What had been his head
Was now a summit, and his bones became stones.
Then every part grew to an enormous size—
For you gods wished it so—and the entire sky
With all its many stars now rested upon him.

Aeolus, son of Hippotas, had confined the winds
Under Mount Etna, and the Morning Star,   740
Who rouses us to work, shone brightest of all
In the eastern sky. Perseus strapped on
His feathered sandals, slung on his scimitar,
And cut through the pure air in a blur of winged feet.
Leaving in his wake innumerable nations,
He now had a clear view of Ethiopia
And the lands of Cepheus. There Jupiter Ammon
Had unjustly ordered that innocent Andromeda
Pay the penalty for the arrogant tongue
Of her mother Cassiopeia.
                              When Perseus,   750
Abas' great-grandson, first saw her chained to the rock,
He might have thought she was a marble statue,
Except that a light breeze was rippling her hair,
And warm tears flowed down from her eyes. Perseus
Was stunned. Entranced by the vision
Of the beauty before him, he almost forgot
To keep beating his wings. As soon as he had landed,

He said,
      "Surely you do not deserve these bonds,
But those that tie true lovers together. Please,
Tell me your name, and the name of your country,   760
And tell me why you are wearing these chains."

At first she was silent, a virgin not daring
To address a man, and out of modesty
She would have hidden her face with her hands
If they had not been fastened behind her.
All she could do was let her eyes fill with tears.
Only when he had asked again and again,
And only because she did not wish to create
The impression of concealing a fault of her own,
Did she tell him her name, the name of her country,   770
And how overconfident her mother was
In her own beauty. The girl was still speaking,
When the sea roared, and a monster rose from the deep,
Breasting the waves as it came toward the shore.
The girl screamed; her grieving father and mother
Stood at her side, both wretched, the mother perhaps
With more justification. They bring no aid,
Only tears and laments to suit the occasion
As they clasp her fettered body. Then the stranger speaks:

"There will be plenty of time for tears later,   780
But only a brief hour to come to the rescue.
If I asked for this girl's hand as Perseus,
Son of Jupiter and that imprisoned Danaë
Whom the god impregnated with his golden rain;
The Perseus who conquered the snake-haired Gorgon;
Who braved the stratosphere on soaring wings—
Surely I would be preferred to all other suitors
As your son-in-law. Now, if the gods favor me,
I will try to add meritorious service
To what else I bring, my bargain being   790
That the girl, saved by my valor, will be mine."

Her parents accept the proposal (who would refuse it?)
And promise a kingdom, as well, for a dowry.

Behold now the monster cutting through the waves
Like a warship driven to ramming speed
By the sweat-covered arms of a crew of rowers.
When it was as far from the cliff as a Balearic sling
Can fire a lead bullet through the air, the young hero
Pushed off hard and ascended high among the clouds.
When the shadow of a man appeared on the water,   800
The sea monster savaged the apparition;
And, as Jupiter's eagle, when it sees a snake
Sunning its mottled back in an open field,
Seizes it from behind, eagerly sinking its talons
Into its scaly neck lest it twist its fangs back,
So the descendant of Inachus, swooping down
Through empty space, attacked the bellowing monster's back,
Poised at its right shoulder, and buried his curved blade
Up to the hilt in its neck. Gravely wounded,
It reared high in the air, then dove underwater,   810
And then turned like a boar when a pack of hounds
Is baying around it. Perseus evaded
The snapping jaws on flashing wings, his scimitar
Slashing the monster wherever it was exposed—
Its barnacled back, its ribcage, and where its spine
Tapered into the tail of a fish. The beast belches
Seawater mixed with purple blood, and Perseus' wings
Are becoming so soggy with all the spume
That he can no longer trust them. He spots
A ledge exposed when the sea is calm, but hidden   820
Whenever the waves run high. He steadies himself here,
Taking hold of the rock face with his left hand,
And plunges his sword three times and once more
Into the monster's gut.
                        The shore is filled
With wild applause that reaches the heavens.
Cassiopeia and Cepheus rejoice
And hail Perseus as their son-in-law,

The pillar of their household and its savior.
Forth from her chains steps Andromeda unbound,
The motive for Perseus' feat and the prize.   830
The victor washes his hands in a basin of water,
And so the hard sand won't hurt that viperous face,
He makes a bed of leaves, strews seaweed on top,
And rests upon this the head of Medusa,
Daughter of Phorcys. The seaweed's porous tendrils
Absorb the monster's power and congeal,
Taking on a new stiffness in their stems and leaves.
The sea nymphs test this wonder on more tendrils
And, delighted to find the result confirmed,
Scatter these tendrils as seeds in the sea.   840
Even now coral has retained this property,
So that its stems, pliant under water,
Turn to stone once exposed to the air.

Perseus now builds three turf altars, one for each
Of three gods: the left for Mercury, the right
For you, virgin warrior, the center for Jove.
He sacrifices a heifer to Minerva,
A calf to the winged god, and to you,
O greatest of gods, a bull. Then he claims
Andromeda, without a dowry, as the reward   850
For his heroic act. Hymen and Amor
Shake the marriage torches; the fires are fed
With rich incense; flowers hang from the roofs;
Lyre, flute, and chorales permeate the air,
Giving sweet testimony of joyful hearts.
The massive double doors swing open to reveal
The golden central court with tables already set,
And noble Ethiopians stream in to the banquet.

When they had finished the feast and their spirits
Were swimming in wine, Bacchus' generous gift,   860
Perseus inquired about the local customs,
Who the people were and what they were like.
The guest who answered said to him in turn,

"Now tell us, Perseus, by what prowess, what arts,
You made off with that head and its curls of snakes?"

And so the hero in the line of Agenor
Told them about a cave hidden in the rock
Under the frozen slopes of Atlas. At its entrance
The Graiae lived, twin daughters of Phorcys,
Who shared the use of a single eye, which the hero   870
Cleverly stole as they passed it back and forth.
Then he made his way through trackless lands,
A barren landscape of blasted trees and rocks,
To where the Gorgons lived. In the fields there
And along the paths he saw the shapes of men
And of animals who had been changed to stone
By Medusa's gaze. But he managed to glimpse
Her dread form reflected in the polished bronze
Of a circular shield strapped to his left arm.
And while the snakes and Medusa herself   880
Were sound asleep, he severed her head from her neck,
And the winged horse Pegasus and his brother,
The warrior Chrysaor, were born from her blood.

He went on to tell of his long journeys
And the dangers he faced—all of this true—
The seas and the lands he had seen far below,
And the stars he had brushed with his beating wings.
When he finished his tale they still wanted more,
And one of them asked why Medusa alone
Among her sisters had snakes in her hair.   890
The guest replied:
                    "Here's the reason, a tale in itself.
She was once very beautiful and sought by many,
And was admired most for her beautiful hair.
I met someone who recalled having seen her.
They say that Neptune, lord of the sea,
Violated her in a temple of Minerva.
The goddess hid her chaste eyes behind her aegis,
But so that the crime would not go unpunished,

She changed the Gorgon's hair to loathsome snakes,
Which the goddess now, to terrify her enemies 900
With numbing fear, wears on her breastplate."

[No selections from Book 5 are included.]

Book 6

The Contest of Arachne and Minerva

Musing on the theme of righteous indignation,
The goddess Minerva turned her mind
To the fate of Arachne of Maeonia,
Who she heard would not yield to her the glory
In the art of working wool. The girl was not famed
For where she was from or who her family was,   10
Only for her art. Her father Idmon of Colophon
Used to dye the wool for her with Phocaean purple.
Her mother was dead. She was a commoner herself,
As was her husband. Nevertheless, Arachne
Had made a name for herself throughout Lydia
Although she came from a small, humble house
And lived in a small town called Hypaepa.
The nymphs would often leave their vineyards
On Mount Tmolus to see her wondrous work,
And the naiads of Pactolus would leave their waters,   20
And it was a joy to see not just her finished fabrics,
But to see them being made, to see such grace and skill.
Whether she was winding up a ball of rough yarn,
Or pressing it with her fingers, or teasing out
Clouds of wool to spin into a long, soft thread,
Or twirling the spindle with a light touch of her thumb,
Or embroidering with her needle—you would know
She had been taught by Pallas. Yet she denied it,
Offended by the notion that she had a teacher,
Even one so great. "Let's have a contest," she said.   30
"There is nothing I wouldn't forfeit if I lose."

So Pallas showed up looking like an old woman,
Grey at the temples, limping in on a staff,
And started to talk.

"Old age does have some things
We shouldn't shun; experience comes with long years.
Don't spurn my advice. Seek all the fame you want
In mortal society for working with wool,
But yield to the goddess, and humbly beg her pardon
For what you said. She will pardon you if you ask."

Arachne glowered at her. Dropping the thread   40
She had been spinning, she could barely hold back
From slapping the old woman, and with undisguised
Anger in her face, answered the disguised goddess,

"You doddering old fool, coming in here like this.
You've lived too long, is your problem. Go talk
To your daughter-in-law, your daughter, whatever.
I've got enough good sense, and just so you'll know
You didn't do any good with all your advice,
I haven't changed my mind. Why does your goddess avoid
A contest with me? Why doesn't she come herself?"   50

"She has!" said the goddess, shedding her disguise
To reveal Pallas Athena. The nymphs
Worshipped her divinity, as did the Mygdonian women.
Arachne alone was unafraid, although she did jump up,
And a sudden blush marked her unwilling cheeks
And then faded away, as the sky turns dark pink
When dawn first appears, and after a little while pales
When the sun comes up. But she persists in her folly,
Eager to win the prize. The daughter of Jupiter
Does not decline, issue any more warnings,   60
Or delay the contest a bit. They set up identical looms
In separate places and stretch out the fine warp.
The web is bound to the beam, a reed separates
The threads of the warp, and the weft is threaded through
By the sharp shuttles worked by their fingers.
Once drawn through the warp, the threads of the weft
Are beaten down into place by the comb's notched teeth.
They each worked quickly, with their clothes tucked in

And tied under their breasts, moving their trained hands
With so much enthusiasm it didn't seem like work.   70
Threads dyed purple in bronze Tyrian vats
Are woven in, and lighter colors shade gradually off.
Just as after a rainstorm, when the sun strikes through,
A long curving bow will tint the vast sky,
And though a thousand colors are shining there,
The eye cannot see the transitions between them,
So too the adjacent threads seem the same color,
But those far apart look different. They worked in
Threads of gold too, telling ancient tales in the weaving.

Pallas depicts the hill of Mars in Athens   80
And that old dispute over naming the city.
Twelve celestials, with Jove in the middle,
Sit on high thrones in august majesty.
Each god has his own distinctive appearance.
Jupiter is royal. The sea god stands with his trident
Striking a cliff, and seawater pours from the broken rock,
His claim to the city. To herself the goddess gives
A shield, a spear, a helmet for her head,
And the aegis protects her breast. And she pictures
A pale-green olive tree laden with fruit   90
Sprouting from the earth where her spear has struck.
The gods look on in awe; Victory crowns her work.

Then, to teach her rival by choice examples
What prize to expect for her outrageous daring,
She weaves four contests in the web's four corners,
Miniature designs each with its own colors.

One corner shows Rhodope and Haemus,
Icy peaks in Thrace that were once mortal beings
Who assumed the names of the gods on high.
Another corner shows the miserable fate   100
Of the queen of the pygmies, defeated by Juno
And transformed by her into a crane
And ordered to fight against her own people.

And she pictures Antigone, whom Juno changed
Into a bird for having the gall to compete
With great Jupiter's consort. Neither Ilium,
Her city, nor her father Laomedon
Could help her now, a stork with white feathers
Applauding herself with her clattering beak.
The last corner shows Cinyras, bereft.   110
Clasping the temple steps that were once the limbs
Of his own daughters, he lies on the stone and weeps.

She bordered it all with peaceful olive wreaths
And with her own tree brought the work to an end.

Arachne depicts Europa deceived by the false bull,
But you would think the bull real, and the water too.
She looks back at the shore and calls to her friends,
And, afraid of the waves, tucks up her dainty feet.
She made Asterië struggling in the eagle's claws,
And Leda lying beneath the swan's wings.   120
She showed how Jove, imaged as a satyr,
Filled lovely Antiope with twin offspring,
And how as Amphitryon he cheated you, Alcmena;
Tricked Danaë as gold, Aegina as fire,
Mnemosyne as a shepherd, and Deo's daughter
As a mottled snake.   She showed you also, Neptune,
As a snorting bull with an Aeolian girl,
As Enipeus begetting the Aloidae,
And deceiving Bisaltis in the shape of a ram.
The golden-haired mother of the grain, Ceres,   130
Knew you as a horse; the snake-haired mother
Of the winged horse had you as a winged bird;
And Melantho as a dolphin.
                              Arachne gave each
A local setting and a face. Here is Phoebus
As a farmer; here he is in hawk feathers,
Here in a skin of a lion; here he's a shepherd
Deceiving Macareus' daughter Isse.

Here we have Bacchus tricking Erigone
With a false bunch of grapes, and here Saturn
As a horse engendering Chiron, the centaur.   140
The narrow border running around the edge
Has flowers intertwined with clinging ivy.

Neither Pallas, nor Envy personified,
Could carp at that work. The golden virago,
Incensed at Arachne's spectacular success,
Ripped the fabric apart with all its embroidery
Of celestial crimes. And, as she had in her hand
A shuttle made of Cytorian boxwood,
She used it to box Arachne's ears. The poor girl
Could not endure this, and she slipped a noose   150
Around her neck. As she was hanging,
Pallas lifted her in pity and said,
                              "Live on,
Wicked girl, but keep hanging, your legacy
(So you will always be wary) to your offspring
For all posterity."
                    And as the goddess left
She sprinkled her with extracts of Hecate's herb.
Touched by this potion, the girl's hair fell off
Along with her nose and ears. Her head became
Her smallest part, and her body small, too,
With her slender fingers clinging to it as legs.   160
The rest was belly, from which she still spins thread
And plies as a spider her old art of weaving.

★ ★ ★

Procne and Philomela

Pandion, king of Athens, formed an alliance
With Tereus of Thrace, a descendant of Mars,
By wedding him to his daughter Procne.
But neither Juno, the bridal goddess,   490
Nor Hymen attended. The Furies lit the way
With torches stolen from a funeral, and

The Furies made their bed. An eerie screech owl
Brooded and sat on the roof of their chamber.
Under this omen Procne and Tereus
Were married, and they conceived their child
Under this omen. Thrace, to be sure, rejoiced,
And the couple thanked the gods, both on the day
When Pandion's daughter married the king
And on the day Itys was born. We never know   500
Where our true advantage lies.

                    Now the Titan Sun
Had led the year through five autumnal seasons,
When Procne, using all her charm, said to Tereus,

"If I am pleasing to you, either send me
To visit my sister, or have my sister come here.
You can tell my father that he will have her back
After a brief stay. It will mean a lot to me
If you give me a chance to see my sister."

Tereus had his ship hauled to the water,
And entered Athens' harbor under sail and oar,   510
Putting in at the Piraeus. As soon as he came
Into his father-in-law's court, they clasped hands,
Exchanged greetings and began to converse.
He was about to present his wife's request,
Which was why he had come, and to promise
A speedy return of the visiting daughter,
When in walked Philomela, richly dressed,
But richer in beauty. She was like the naiads
We hear about, or dryads walking in the woods,
If only they had elegant clothing like hers.   520
Tereus was inflamed the moment he saw her,
As if one were to set fire to a field of grain,
Or a pile of leaves, or to hay in a loft.
Her beauty was reason enough, but with Tereus
His own libido and the passionate nature
Of men from his region were also factors.
Nature and race both caused him to burn.
His first impulse was to corrupt her attendants,

Or her nurse, and then to tempt the girl herself
With lavish gifts, even if it cost his kingdom,   530
Or perhaps just to carry her off and rape her
And then defend his rape with a bloody war.
Mad with passion, he would dare anything,
And his heart could not contain the fires within.
Impatient now, he repeated Procne's request,
Using her as a pretext to plead his own case.
Love made him eloquent, and as often as
He sounded too urgent, he would say that Procne
Wanted it so. He even threw in some tears,
As if she had ordered that too. Gods above,   540
Men's minds are pitch-black! In the very act
Of constructing his crime, Tereus is credited
With a kind heart and gets praised for his sin.
And what about this? Philomela herself
Has the same wish. She drapes her arms
Upon her father's shoulders and coaxes him
To let her go and visit her sister,
Pleading for (and against) her own well-being.
Tereus gazes at her and paws her by looking;
As he sees her kisses, and sees her arms   550
Around her father's neck, he takes it all in
As fuel for the fire, food for his passion;
And whenever she embraces her father
He wishes he were her father, nor would he be
Any less impious. Pandion is won over
By the pleas of both. Philomela is happy
And thanks her father, poor girl. She thinks
It is a great success for her and her sister,
But it will be sheer agony for both of them.

Now Phoebus had only a little work left,   560
His horses treading the sky's downward slopes.
A royal feast was spread, wine in golden cups,
And then they retired for a good night's sleep.
But although the Thracian king was in bed,
He could not stop thinking about her, recalling

Her looks, the way she moved, her hands,
And what he had not seen he readily imagined,
Feeding his own fires, and he could not sleep.
Dawn came. Pandion, wringing his son-in-law's hand
As he was leaving, committed his daughter   570
To Tereus' care and, with tears welling up, said,

"My dear son, since it is for a good reason,
And both my daughters want it, and you do too,
I give her to you, Tereus, and by your honor
And the ties between us, and by the gods above,
I beg you to watch over her with a father's love,
And to send back as soon as possible
(It will seem forever to me) the sweet solace
Of my anxious old age. And, Philomela,
If you care for me, return as soon as you can.   580
It is enough that your sister is so far away."

He kissed his child good-bye as he said these things,
Gentle tears falling from his eyes the while.
He asked for their right hands as a pledge
And joined them together. And he begged them
To greet his daughter and grandson for him.
Sobbing, choked with tears, he could barely say
His last farewell, and was filled with foreboding.

As soon as Philomela was on his painted ship,
And the oars churned sea, and land drifted away,   590
"I've won!" Tereus shouted. "My answered prayers
Are freight onboard!" The barbarian lout exults,
He can barely defer his pleasures, and he never
Twists his eyes away from her, just like an eagle,
Jove's bird, who has dropped a hare from his talons
Into its high aerie. The captive has no chance
To escape, and the raptor sits eyeing his prey.

The voyage was done; they got off the battered ship,
And Tereus dragged the daughter of Pandion

To a hut in the gloom of an ancient forest   600
Where he shut her in, pale, trembling, afraid
Of everything, and begging with tears to know
Where her sister was. He told her the outrage
He was about to commit and then overpowered her,
One girl, all alone, calling often for her father,
Often for her sister, but above all the great gods.
She trembled like a quivering lamb, who,
After it has been wounded and then spat out
By a grey wolf, cannot yet believe it is safe;
Or like a dove whose feathers are smeared   610
With its own blood and who still shudders with fear
Of those greedy talons that pierced her skin.
When her senses returned she clawed at her hair,
And beat and scratched her arms like a mourner,
And then stretched out her hands as she cried:

"Oh, you horrible monster, what have you done?
Don't you care anything about my father's charges,
His tears, my sister's love, my own virginity
Or the bonds of marriage? You've jumbled it all up!
I've become my sister's whorish rival, and you   620
A husband to us both! Procne now must be
My enemy. Why don't you just kill me,
So there's no crime left for you to commit,
You traitor? I wish you had killed me before
That unspeakable bedding! Then my shade
Would have been innocent. If the gods above
See these things, if there are any gods at all,
If all things have not perished with me, then,
Sooner or later, you will pay for this!
I will shrug off shame and tell everyone   630
What you have done. I'll go to the marketplace
If I can, and if I'm shut up in these woods,
I'll fill the woods with my story and move
Even the rocks to pity. Heaven's air will hear it,
And if there's any god there he'll hear it too."

Tereus' savage, tyrannical wrath
Was aroused by her words, and his fear no less.
He drew his sword from its sheath, caught her by the hair
And tied her hands behind her back. When she saw the sword
Philomela offered her throat, hoping for death.   640
But he gripped her protesting tongue with pincers
As it kept calling her father's name and cut it off,
Still struggling to speak, with his pitiless blade.
The root writhed in her throat; the tongue itself
Lay quivering on the dark earth, murmuring low;
And, as the tail of a snake twitches when severed,
So too her tongue, and with its last dying spasm
It sought its mistress' feet. Even after this atrocity
He is said to have gone back—it strains belief—
Again and again to her torn body in lust.   650

And then he had the nerve to go back to Procne,
Who, as soon as she saw her husband, asked
Where her sister was. He forced a groan
And made up a story about how she had died.
His tears made it plausible. Then Procne
Tore from her shoulders the robe that shone
With a broad gold border, and, dressed now in black,
Built an empty tomb and made pious offerings
To shades that were not, and mourned her sister's fate
In a way that her fate should not have been mourned.   660

And now the sun god has passed through twelve
Zodiacal signs again. What can Philomela do?
A guard precludes flight, the hut's walls are stone,
Mute lips cannot tell. But grief has its own genius,
And with trouble comes cunning. She sets up
A Thracian web on a loom, and weaves purple signs
Onto a white background, revealing the crime.
When it is done she gives the woven fabric
To her sole attendant and asks her with gestures
To take it to the queen. She takes it to Procne   670

Without knowing the inner message it bears.
The tyrant's wife unrolls the cloth and reads
The strands of her sister's song of lament,
And (a wonder that she could) says nothing.
Grief seals her mouth, and her tongue cannot find
Words indignant enough. There is no room for tears,
But she rushes ahead to confound right and wrong,
And all she can do is imagine her vengeance.

It was the time when the Thracian women
Celebrate the twice-yearly festival of Bacchus.   680
Night witnesses the rituals. Mount Rhodope
Rings at night with loud, tingling bronze.
So it is by night that the queen goes forth
Equipped for the god's rites and arrayed for frenzy,
Her head wreathed with vines, a deerskin hanging
From her left side, a light spear on her shoulder.
She streaks through the woods with an attendant throng,
Procne in her rage, driven on by grief's fury,
And mimicking yours, Bacchus. She comes at last
To the hut deep in the woods, and shrieks "Euhoë!"   690
She breaks down the doors, seizes her sister,
Dresses her as a Bacchant, and hiding her face
In ivy leaves, leads the stunned girl into her house.

When Philomela saw that she had been brought
To that accursed house, the poor girl trembled
And the color drained from her face. Procne
Found a good place, took off all the ritual garb,
And, unveiling her sister's embarrassed face,
She took her in her arms. But Philomela
Could not lift her eyes to her, seeing herself   700
As having betrayed her sister. Looking down
And wanting to swear, to call the gods as witness
That her shame was forced upon her, she used her hands
In place of her voice. But Procne is burning,
Unable to control her rage, and scolds her sister

For her weeping.
              "This is no time for tears," she said,
"But for steel, or, if you have it, something stronger
Than steel. I am ready for any crime, sister,
Either to burn this palace down and throw Tereus,
Whose fault all this is, into the flames,   710
Or to cut out his tongue and eyes and the parts
That stole your chastity and squeeze his guilty soul
Out through a thousand wounds. I am prepared
For some great deed; I just don't know what."

While Procne was saying these things, Itys
Came in to his mother. She now realized
What she could do, and looking at the boy
With pitiless eyes, said,
               "Ah, how much
You look like your father."
                    And saying no more,
She planned a grim deed in her seething rage.   720
But when the child came up to greet his mother
And he put his small arms around her neck,
Kissing and charming her as little boys do,
The mother in her was moved, her anger dissolved,
And she began to shed tears in spite of herself.
But when she felt herself wavering through excess
Of maternal love, she turned toward her sister's face
And then back and forth between both of them.

"One coos, the other has no tongue with which to speak.
He calls me mother; why can't she call me sister?   730
Look at whose wife you are, daughter of Pandion!
Will you disgrace your husband? But fidelity
To a husband like Tereus is criminal."

And she dragged Itys off as if she were a tigress
Dragging a suckling fawn through the Ganges' dark woods.
When they reached a remote part of the great house

And the boy saw his fate, he stretched out his hands,
Screaming, "Mother! Mother!" and tried to put his arms
Around her neck. Procne struck him in the side
With a sword, and did not change her expression.   740
This one wound was fatal, but Philomela
Slit his throat also, and they sliced up the body
Still warm with life. Some pieces boil in bronze kettles,
Some hiss on spits, and the room drips with gore.

To this feast Procne invites Tereus,
All unknowing. She pretends that the meal
Is a sacred Athenian custom,
And that only the husband may partake,
And she removes all the attendants and slaves.
So Tereus sits on his high, ancestral throne   750
And stuffs his belly with his own flesh and blood.
So great is his mind's blindness that he cries,
"Get Itys here!" Procne cannot conceal
Her cruel joy, and eager to be the herald
Of her butchery, "You have him inside,"
She says. He looks around, asks where he is,
And as he asks again and calls, Philomela,
Just as she was, her hair stained with blood,
Leaps forward and throws the gory head of Itys
Into his father's face, nor was there ever a time   760
When she longed more to be able to speak
And proclaim her joy in words that matched it.
The Thracian overturns the table with a roar
And calls upon the viperish Furies of Styx.
If only now he could lay open his chest
And draw out the feast, vomit his son's flesh.
But all he can do is weep, and call himself
His son's wretched tomb. Then he draws his sword
And pursues the two daughters of Pandion.
You would think that the two Athenians' bodies   770
Were poised on wings, and poised on wings they were,
Philomela flying off to the woods
As a nightingale, and Procne as a swallow

Rising up to the eaves. And even now their breasts
Retain the marks of the slaughter, and their feathers
Are stained with blood. Tereus' desire for vengeance,
And his grief, made him swift, and he himself
Was changed into a bird, with a crest on his head
And an outsized beak instead of a sword.
He is the hoopoe, a bird that seems to be armed.   780

★ ★ ★

Book 7

★ ★ ★

Procris and Cephalus

*[Having sailed to Aegina by the power of the East Wind to secure military
assistance against Crete, the Athenian prince Cephalus and two younger
Athenians, the sons of Pallas, awaken after enjoying a day of talk and
feasting with their hosts, King Aeacus and his son Phocus.]*

When the golden sun lifted his crest of light,
The East Wind still blew, keeping the ships
From sailing back home. The two sons of Pallas
Came to Cephalus, who was older, and together
They went to see the king, but he was still fast asleep.   730
Aeacus' son Phocus met them at the door,
For Telamon and his brother Peleus
Were marshaling the troops. Phocus led the Athenians
Into a beautiful inner courtyard
And there the four of them sat down together.
Phocus noticed that Cephalus had in his hand
A javelin made out of an unusual wood
And tipped in gold. After saying a few words,
He interrupted himself:

      "I love the woods
And am a hunter myself, but I've been wondering   740
What kind of wood that javelin is made of.
If it were ash, it would have a tawny color,
And if it were cornel it would be knotty.
I don't recognize the wood, but I've never seen
A javelin more beautiful than the one you have."

One of the Athenian brothers replied,

"You'll like its use more than its looks. It goes
Straight to the target, no luck involved,
And comes back bloodied all on its own."

Young Phocus wanted to know all about it then,   750
Where it came from, and who gave Cephalus
Such a wonderful gift. Cephalus told him
What he wanted to know, but was ashamed to say
What that javelin cost him. He fell silent,
Then, thinking of his lost wife, burst into tears.

"Who could believe that it is this weapon
That makes me weep? And it will make me weep
All the rest of my life. This javelin destroyed me
Along with my dear wife. I wish I'd never had it.
My wife was Procris. You may have heard of   760
Orithyia, the beauty ravaged by the North Wind;
She was her sister, and if you were to compare
The two sisters in character and beauty,
Procris would be more worthy to be stolen away.
Erechtheus gave her to me in marriage,
But Love tied the knot. I was called happy,
And I was. I might have still been happy now,
But the gods saw it differently.

                              In the second month
After our wedding, while I was spreading my nets
To catch antlered deer, Aurora, golden in her dawn,   770
Had just dispelled the shadows when she saw me
From the top of flowering Hymettus
And took me against my will. May the goddess
Not be offended if I speak the truth,
But as sure as her face is lovely as a rose,
As sure as she holds the border of day and night
And drinks nectar, it was Procris I loved,
Procris in my heart, Procris ever on my lips.
I kept talking about our wedding and the first time
We made love in our now desolate bed.   780
The goddess was upset and said,

　　　　　　　　　　　　　　　'Quit complaining,
You little ingrate. Keep your Procris! But if I can
Prophesy at all, you'll wish you never had her.'

And mad as can be, she sent me back to her.
As I made my way home the goddess' warning
Kept going through my mind, and I began to fear
That my wife had not kept her marriage vows.
Her youth and beauty made adultery credible,
But her morals made it unthinkable.
Still, I'd been gone a long time, and the goddess I'd left　　　790
Was a shining example of infidelity herself, and,
Well, we lovers fear everything. I decided
To create a grievance for myself by tempting
Her fidelity with gifts. Aurora helped me
With my jealous fear by changing my form
(I felt it happen), and so I entered Athens
Incognito. When I went into my house
There was no sign of guilt anywhere; everyone
Was anxious for the return of their absent lord.
It took all my ingenuity to gain an audience　　　800
With Erechtheus' daughter. When I looked at her
My heart skipped a beat and I almost abandoned
The test of her fidelity that I had planned.
It was all I could do to keep from coming clean
And kissing her as she deserved. She was sad,
But no woman could be more beautiful
Than she was in her sadness, and all of her grief
Was longing for the husband that she had lost.
Imagine, Phocus, how beautiful she was,
How her grief itself made her more beautiful.　　　810
I don't have to tell you how often her chastity
Defeated my attempts, how often she said,

'I keep myself for one man alone; wherever he is,
All my joy is for him.'
　　　　　　　　　　What man in his right mind
Would need more proof than that? But no,

I wasn't satisfied, and wound up hurting myself.
By promising fortunes for one night with her
And then promising more, I made her hesitate,
And then, gloating in my false victory, I exclaimed,

'Ha! There's no adulterer here, but your real husband,   820
And I've caught you betraying me.'
                                        She said nothing.
In total silence, overcome with shame, she fled
Her pathetic husband, left his treacherous house.
Loathing me and hating the entire male race
She took to the mountains and followed Diana.
Alone, I felt love burning deep in my bones.
I begged forgiveness, confessed that I had sinned,
Admitted that I too might have succumbed
If someone had offered me gifts like that.
When I said these things and she had avenged   830
Her outraged sense of self-respect, she came back,
And spent sweet years with me, two hearts as one.
Then, as if she herself were too slight a gift,
She gave me a hound that she had received
From her own Cynthia, and said that this dog
Would outrun any other. And she gave me also
A javelin, the one you see in my hands.
Would like to hear the story of both gifts?
It is a strange tale, and you will be moved.

After Oedipus had solved the riddle of the Sphinx   840
She plunged to her death, and the dark prophetess lay
Forgetful of her mysterious sayings.
But Themis does not allow such things
To go unpunished, and a second monster
Was promptly dispatched to Aonian Thebes.
The whole countryside lived in constant terror
Of this beast, fearing for themselves and their herds,
And so all of us neighboring young heroes
Surrounded the wide fields with our hunting nets.
Well, she just sailed right over the top of the nets   850

With one light leap and then kept on going.
We unleashed the hounds, but she made fools
Out of the entire pack, leaving them all behind
As if she had wings. Then all of the hunters,
Myself included, called for Whirlwind (my dog's name).
He was already straining to slip free of his chain,
And as soon as he was released we couldn't tell
Where he might be. You could see his prints in the dust,
But that dog was gone. No spear is faster,
No bullet whirled from a sling, no reed arrow   860
Shot from a Gortynian bow. I climbed up
To the top of a hill that overlooked the plain
To get a better view of that amazing chase.
The wild thing looked like it was almost caught
And then would slip right out of the dog's open jaws,
And she was cunning, wouldn't run in a straight line,
But would feint and then wheel sharply around
To make her enemy lose his momentum.
Lailaps pressed her hard, matching her speed,
But just when you thought he had her,   870
His jaws would snap on empty air. I went
To my javelin, and just as I had it balanced
And was twisting my fingers into the loop,
I glanced away, and when I turned my eyes back,
I saw two marble statues out on the plain.
Incredible. One of them you'd swear was running away
And the other was about to catch its prey.
If there was any god with them in that race,
That god must have wanted neither to lose."

Cephalus fell silent. Phocus asked,
                              "What then   880
Do you have against the javelin?"
                              So Cephalus
Told him what he had against the javelin.

"My sorrow began in joy, son of Aeacus,
And it is a joy now to recall that blessed time,

Those years when I was happy with my wife,
As is only right, and she with her husband.
Mutual cares and shared love bound us together.
She would not have preferred Jupiter's love
To mine, and no woman could have taken me
Away from her, not even Venus herself.   890
We were passionately in love with each other.

When the rising sun struck the mountains' peaks
I used to go hunting in the woods. I was young,
And I went out alone, no attendants with me,
No horses, no dogs on the scent, no knotted nets.
I was safe with my javelin. And when I had my fill
Of bringing down game, I would look for shade
And the breeze gently stirring in the cool valleys.
I looked for that soft breeze in the summer heat,
Waited for the breeze, relief from my labors.   900
'Come, Aura,' I remember I used to croon,
'Help me out, blow on my chest, you know
I love you, cool down my heat as only you can.'
And I might, since my fates were drawing me on,
Add some sweet nothings, saying things like.
'You're my greatest pleasure,' and 'You make me feel
So good. I'm crazy about the woods because of you.
I just love to feel your breath on my face.'
Someone overhearing this mistook its meaning,
And thought that by 'Aura' I meant not the breeze   910
But some nymph, that I was in love with a nymph.
This tattletale went to Procris with a story
That I had been unfaithful and whispered to her
The words he had heard. Love is a credulous thing.
She was overwhelmed and, I heard, fainted
And only came to after a long time, weeping
And cursing her fate, complaining about
My supposed infidelity. Deeply troubled
By an imaginary crime, she feared what was nothing,
A name with nothing behind it, the poor woman,   920
Grieving as if 'Aura' were an actual rival.

Yet she often thought, in her misery,
That she might be wrong and said she would not
Believe it, would not condemn her husband,
Until she saw it herself.
                          The next morning,
As soon as Aurora had dispelled the dark,
I went out into the woods, and after a good hunt
I lay in the grass, and as I was calling, 'Aura,
Come relieve my suffering,' I thought I heard
Someone moaning. Still, I went on, 'Come, dearest.'   930
The fallen leaves rustled in reply. Thinking
It was a wild animal, I threw my javelin.
It was Procris, clasping her wounded breast
And crying out, 'Ah, me.' Recognizing
My wife's voice, I ran frantically toward the sound.
I found her half alive, her clothes spattered with blood
And trying to pull the spear, this spear that she gave me,
Out from the wound. What misery. I lifted
Her body, dearer to me than my own,
As gently as I could, tore the clothes from her breast   940
And tried to stop the bleeding, begging her
Not to leave me guilty of her death. Dying,
And with little strength left, she still forced herself
To speak a few words, saying,
                          'By the bed
We swore to share, by the gods I pray to above
And by my own gods, by any good I deserve of you,
And by the love that even in death remains
And is the cause of my death, do not allow
This Aura to replace me.'
                          It was then I realized,
Too late, the error the name caused, and told her.   950
But what good did it do to tell her? She sank back,
Her last bit of strength ebbing away with her blood.
While her eyes could still focus on something,
She looked at me, and breathed out on my lips
Her unfortunate spirit, but as she died
Her face at last seemed to be free from care."

The hero had finished his story in tears
When Aeacus came in with his other two sons
And an army of newly enlisted men
That he presented to Cephalus, all heavily armed.   960

Book 8

★ ★ ★

Minos and the Minotaur

[Minos, king of Crete and the son of Jove and Europa, returns home after conquering the Athenians. Sometime earlier, his wife Pasiphaë had mated with a bull and borne the Minotaur.]

Minos paid his vows to Jove, a hundred bulls,
As soon as he set foot on the beach in Crete
And adorned his palace with the spoils of war.
But now the family disgrace had grown up
And its mother's sordid adultery was revealed
In the strange hybrid monster. Minos intended
To remove this shame from his chambers and enclose it   190
In a dark, winding labyrinth. Daedalus,
A renowned master architect, did the work,
Confounding the usual lines of sight
With a maze of conflicting passageways.
Just as the Maeander plays in Phrygian fields,
Flowing back and forth and winding around
In its ambiguous course so that sometimes it sees
Its own waters flowing toward it, and flows itself
Now back toward its source, now toward the sea—
So Daedalus made all those passageways wander,   200
And he himself had a hard time finding his way
Back to the entrance of the deceptive building.

After Minos had shut up the Minotaur there
He fed him twice on Athenian blood,
Once every nine years. But the third tribute
Of Athenian youths was the creature's undoing,

And when Theseus, with Ariadne's help,
Found his way back to the difficult entrance—
Which no previous hero had ever done—
By winding up the thread, he took Minos' daughter   210
And sailed for Dia, and then abandoned her
On that island's shore. Marooned and reciting
A litany of complaints, she received the aid
And love of Bacchus, and so that she might shine
Among the eternal stars, he took the tiara
That circled her brow and sent it off to the sky.
It flew through the thin air, and as it flew
Its gemstones were changed into gleaming fires
That found their place, still in the shape of a Crown,
Between Ophiouchus' and Hercules' stars.   220

Daedalus and Icarus

Daedalus, meanwhile, hating his long exile
In Crete, and longing for the place of his birth,
Was locked in by the sea.
                    "He may block
Land and sea," he said, "but the sky is open;
We will go that way. Minos may own everything,
But he does not own the air."
                    And turning his mind
Toward unknown arts, he transformed nature.

Spreading out feathers, he arranged them in order
From shortest to longest, as if climbing a slope,
The way reeds once rose into a panpipe's shape.   230
Then he bound the midline of the quills with thread
And the ends with wax, and bent the formation
Into a slight curve, imitating a real bird's wing.
His son Icarus stood at his side, and, unaware
That he was touching his peril, the beaming boy
Would try to catch feathers blown by the breeze,
Or would knead the yellow wax with his thumb
And as he played generally get in the way
Of his genius father at work. When he had put

The finishing touches on his craft, the artisan   240
Suspended himself between two identical wings,
And his body hovered in the moving air.
Then he equipped his son, saying,
                                        "Stay in the middle,
Icarus. I warn you, if you go lower
The water will weigh down the feathers; higher,
The sun's heat will scorch them. Fly in between,
And don't gawk at Boötes, the Dipper,
Or the sword of Orion! Pick out your path
By following me."
                            He gave him flying instructions
While fitting the unfamiliar wings to his shoulders,   250
And what with the work and the admonitions
His old cheeks grew moist, and his father's hands trembled.
He kissed his dear son, a kiss never to be repeated,
And rising on wings he flies ahead in fear
For his companion—like a bird who leads
Its tender young into the air from its aerial nest—
Urging him to follow, teaching him ruinous arts,
And beating his own wings as he looks back at his son.
A fisherman with a trembling rod sees them—
Or a shepherd leaning on his staff, or a plowman—   260
They gape at these beings negotiating the air
And take them for gods. Juno's isle Samos
Is now on the left (Delos and Paros are long gone)
And on the right are Lebinthos and honeyed Calymne,
When the boy begins to enjoy this daring flight
And veers off from his leader. He is drawn to the sky
And goes higher. Proximity to the blazing sun
Softens the scented wax that bound the feathers,
And the wax melts. He beats his naked arms
But lacking plumage cannot purchase air,   270
And his mouth was shouting his father's name
When the blue water, which takes its name from his,
Closed over the boy. His bereft father,
A father no more, cried "Icarus, where are you,
Icarus, where should I look for you?" and kept calling,

"Icarus." Then he saw the feathers in the waves.
He swore off his arts and buried the body,
And the land is known by the name on the tomb.

Meleager and the Calydonian Boar

Now Sicily received the weary Daedalus,
Where Cocalus defended the suppliant
And was thought of as kind. And now, too, Athens
Stopped paying the grim tribute, thanks to Theseus.
They wreathe the temple, call on Minerva,
The warrior goddess, and upon Jupiter,
And worship all gods with blood sacrifices,   310
Bestowing gifts upon them and burning incense.
Theseus' fame spread through all the Greek cities,
And all Achaea sought his help in times of peril.
Calydon too, although she had her own Meleager,
Anxiously begged for his help.
      The cause of the trouble
Was a boar, servant and avenger of an outraged Diana.
They say that Oeneus, king of Calydon,
Giving thanks for a bounteous harvest,
Offered the firstfruits to Ceres, wine to Bacchus,
And poured to blond Pallas libations of oil.   320
From the rural deities to the gods of high heaven,
Each received due honor. Only Diana's altar
Was left without incense. Gods can get really angry.

"This will not go unpunished," she said to herself.
Although we may be unhonored, it will not be said
We are unavenged."
     And the scorned goddess sent
An avenging boar through Oeneus' fields,
A boar as big as the bulls that graze in Epirus,
Bigger than Sicilian bulls. His eyes blazed
With blood and fire; he had a long, thick neck;   330

His bristles were like a forest of spear shafts;
His hoarse grunts came out with steaming foam
That lathered his shoulders; his tusks were as long
As an Indian elephant's; lightning issued
From his mouth, and his breath burned vegetation.
He tramples the green shoots of the growing grain,
And now he destroys the mature crop of a farmer
Doomed to mourn, cutting off the ripe ears.
Entire vineyards heavy with grapes are leveled
And branches with their olives are ripped from trees.   340
He savages cattle too. Neither shepherds nor dogs
Can protect their flocks, nor bulls their herds.
The people run off everywhere and don't feel safe
Except behind city walls.
     Finally Meleager
And a picked band of young heroes assembled,
Bound for glory:
     The twin sons of Leda,
The boxer Pollux and Castor the horseman;
Jason, who built the first ship; the best friends
Theseus and Pirithoüs; the two sons of Thestius;
Lynceus and swift Idas, sons of Aphareus;   350
Caeneus, no longer a woman; fierce Leucippus
And Acastus the spearman; Hippothoös
And Dryas; Amyntor's son Phoenix;
Actor's two sons and Elean Phyleus.
Telamon was there too, and great Achilles' father;
Admetus, son of Pheres, and Boeotian Iolaus,
Impulsive Eurytion, Echion the great runner;
Locrian Lelex, Panopeus, Hyleus
And ferocious Hippasus; Nestor, who was then
In the prime of his life; those whom Hippocoön   360
Sent from ancient Amyclae; Laertes,
Penelope's father-in-law; Arcadian Ancaeus;
Ampycus' son, the prophet Mopsus; Amphiaraus,
Oecleus' son, not yet undone by his wife;
And Atalanta, pride of the Arcadian woods.
A polished pin fastened her robe at the neck,

Her hair was pulled back in a simple knot.
Her arrows rattled in an ivory quiver
Hanging from her left shoulder, and her left hand
Held her bow. That was how she was dressed.   370
Her face was one that you could truly say
Was girlish for a boy and for a girl boyish.
For Meleager it was love at first sight
(Denied by a deity), and he felt the heat,
Saying to himself, "What a lucky guy
If that girl ever says yes." It was not the time—
And he was embarrassed—for him to say more.
The great contest was about to begin.

There was a virgin forest, dense and primeval,
Running from the plain to the slope of a valley.   380
When the heroes reached it, some stretched the nets,
Others slipped the dogs from their leashes, and some
Followed the boar's well-marked trail, eager to meet
Their mortal peril. At the bottom of the valley
The rainwater drained into a marshy spot
Overgrown with willows, swamp grass, and rushes
And with an undergrowth of reeds. It was from here
The boar was flushed out and came at his tormentors
Like lightning from a cloud. The grove was laid low
By his charge, and the battered trees crashed   390
As the heroes yelled and clenched their spears
With their broad iron heads pointed toward the boar.
He kept coming, scattering the baying dogs
With sidelong thrusts of his tusks as one by one
They tried to impede his furious onrush.
Echion cast first, but his throw was wasted.
The spear sticking lightly in a maple tree.
The next, thrown by Jason, would have pierced
The boar's back, but had too much force and went long.
Then Mopsus prayed,
           "Apollo, if I have ever and still do   400
Worship you, let my spear hit its mark."
                The god did his best

To answer his prayer. The boar was hit but uninjured.
Diana had snapped the iron off from the spear in flight
And the shaft arrived without any point.
The beast's anger now burned no less gently than lightning.
Fire gleamed from his eye and breathed from his throat,
And as a huge rock launched by a catapult
Heads toward soldiers stationed on walls and towers,
So too, with that kind of irresistible power, the boar
Rushed on the heroes, flattening Eupalamus   410
And Pelagon, who manned the right wing. Their comrades
Carried them off. But Enaesimus, son of Hippocoön,
Did not escape the boar's fatal stroke. As he turned to run
In terror, he was hamstrung and his muscles failed.
Pylian Nestor would have never made it to Troy,
But with a supreme effort he planted his spear
And vaulted into a tree, from whose branches
He looked down in safety at his enemy below.
He was whetting his tusks on the trunk of an oak,
An ominous sign, and with renewed confidence   420
In his sharpened weapons he sliced through the thigh
Of great Hippasus with a hooking stroke.
And now Castor and Pollux, not yet stars in the sky
But still conspicuous among the rest, came riding up
On horses whiter than snow, pumped their spears
And sent them humming through the air. Both would have
Hit the boar, too, except that that the beast took cover
In a thicket, where neither horse nor spear could follow.
Telamon did try to follow, but got careless and tripped
Over a root, and while Peleus was helping him up   430
Atalanta notched an arrow on the string and let fly.
It grazed the boar's back and stuck beneath his ear,
Staining the bristles red with a trickle of blood.
She was not happier over her shot's success
Than Meleager was. He saw the blood first
And was the first to point it out to his comrades.
"You will be honored," he said, "for this bold achievement!"
The men's faces turned red, and they spurred each other on,
Their spirits rising as they shouted and hurled spears

But in no good order, their very volume preventing   440
Any from hitting the target. Then Ancaeus,
Himself an Arcadian, armed with a battle-axe
And determined to meet his destiny, cried out,

"All right, boys, let's find out how much a man's weapons
Outweigh a girl's. Leave this to me. I don't care
If Diana herself protects this boar with her arrows.
I'm taking this animal down, Diana or not!"

That was his boast, all swollen with pride,
And he lifted the axe overhead with both hands,
Standing on tiptoe and ready to strike. The boar   450
Went for his adversary's most vulnerable spot,
Both tusks slashing fiercely at the top of the groin.
Ancaeus went down, his entrails flowing out
Along with his blood; the ground was soaked with gore.
When Ixion's son Pirithoüs advanced on the enemy
Balancing a hunting spear in his strong right hand,
Theseus called to him,
                          "Back away, O dearer to me
Than I am to myself, half of my soul, stop!
It's all right for the brave to fight from a distance.
Ancaeus' rash valor has done him no good."   460

As he spoke he hurled his heavy hardwood spear
Tipped with bronze, but although it was well thrown
And looked like an answer to all their prayers,
A leafy branch of an oak tree turned it aside.
Then Jason hurled his javelin, which, as it happened,
Swerved off and killed a perfectly good hound,
Passing through his flanks and pinning him down.
But Meleager showed a different hand. He threw
Two spears; one of these punched into the earth,
But the other one stuck in the spine of the beast.   470
While the boar spins around and around in his rage,
Spewing foam and fresh blood, Jason presses on,
Jabbing at him and driving him mad until at last

He buries his hunting spear deep in the shoulder.
The others go wild, shouting applause and crowding around
To clasp hands with the victor. They gaze in wonder
At the huge carcass covering so much ground
And still are not sure it is safe to touch it,
But each of them wets his own spear in its blood.

Then Meleager, standing with his foot   480
Upon that lethal head, spoke to Atalanta:

"Take the spoils, Arcadian, that are mine by right,
And let my glory come in part to you."

And he gave her the spoils, the bristling hide
And the magnificent head with its enormous tusks.
Both the gift and the giver made Atalanta glad,
But an envious murmur rose through the company,
And Thestius' two sons stretched out their arms
And cried in a loud voice,
                              "Back off, girl,
And don't take our honors. And don't be a fool   490
Trusting your beauty, or this lovesick giver
Might not be around for you."
                              And they took
The gift from her and from him the right to give.
This was too much for the son of Mars.
                                        "Learn,"
He said, "You two who plunder another's right,
The difference between a threat and a deed."

And he drained Plexippus' unsuspecting heart
With sinful steel. His brother Toxeus
Stood there hesitating, wanting to avenge
His brother but fearing to share his brother's fate,   500
But Meleager cut short his deliberations.
While the spear was still warm from its prior victim
He warmed it again in his brother's blood.

Althea was bringing gifts to the temple
In thanksgiving for the victory of her son
When she saw her brothers' corpses carried in.
She filled the city with her loud lamentation
And changed her robes from golden to black.
But when she learned who the murderer was
All of her grief became a lust for vengeance. 510

There was a log of wood which, when Althea
Was in labor, the three Fates threw into the fire
As they spun the thread of Meleager's life.

"We give to you," they said, "and to this log
The same span of time."
                          When the three sisters
Had chanted this prophecy and disappeared,
The mother snatched the burning log from the fire
And doused it with water. It had long been hidden
In the depths of the house, and, kept safe there,
Safeguarded your life for years, young hero. 520
Now Meleager's mother brought out this log,
And had her servants pile up pine and kindling.
She lit the unfriendly fire. Four times
She was about to throw the log in the flames,
And four times she stopped. Mother fought sister,
Two names tugging at the one heart she had.
Her cheeks would pale at what she was about to do,
Then her burning anger would glow in her eyes.
At times she was an ominous, threatening figure,
And then you would think her some pitiful thing. 530
And although her anger had dried up her tears,
Tears would still come. It was like a ship
Driven both by the wind and an opposing tide,
Feeling the two forces at work and yielding
Uneasily to both. So too Thestius' daughter
Wavered between her uncertain emotions,
Extinguishing her wrath and fanning it again.

But the sister in her begins to prevail
Over the mother, and to appease with blood
Her blood-relatives' shades, Althea becomes   540
Pious in her impiety. When the pestilential flames
Reached full strength, she said,
                              "Let that pyre
Turn my own flesh to ashes."
                                    And holding
The fateful log in her dire hand, she stood
In her misery before the sepulchral altars
And said:
          "Triple goddesses, vengeful Furies,
Eumenides, turn your faces toward these rites.
I avenge, and I do evil. Death must be atoned by death,
Crime added to crime, funeral to funeral.
May mounded grief destroy this accursed house.   550
Shall Oeneus enjoy his victorious son
And Thestius be childless? Better that both grieve.
But may you, new ghosts of my brothers,
Feel my devotion and accept the sacrifice
I offer to the dead at so great a cost,
The doomed tribute of my own womb. Ah,
Where is this taking me? Brothers, forgive
A mother's heart! My hands cannot finish this.
I confess that he deserves to die, but I cannot bear
To cause his death. But, then, shall he go unscathed,   560
Live victorious, all puffed up with success,
The great lord of Calydon, while the two of you
Are scanty ashes and pale, shivering ghosts?
I will not allow it. Let him die in his malice
And drag to perdition his father's hopes,
His father's kingdom and his fatherland's ruins.
Ah, where is my mother's mind? A parent's care?
The misery I endured for ten long months?
Oh, you should have burned to death as an infant
In that first fire—if only I could have borne it!   570
You lived by my gift; now you will die
For what you have done. Pay the price for it,

And give back the life I gave to you twice,
Once at your birth, once by saving the log—
Or put me on my brothers' pyre too. Oh,
I want to and I can't. What shall I do?
My brothers' wounds are before my eyes now,
All that blood; and now the name of mother
And a mother's love are breaking my heart.
God, I am wretched! It isn't right that you win,   580
Brothers, but go ahead, win! Just let me have
The solace I give you, and let me follow you."

Althea spoke, and as she turned her face away
Her trembling hand dropped the mortal log
Into the flames. It groaned, or seemed to groan,
As it flared up and burned in the unwilling fire.

Far away and knowing nothing of this,
Meleager burns in those flames. Feeling
A scorching fire deep inside his body,
It takes all his courage to master the pain.   590
Yet he grieves that he will die a bloodless
And ignoble death, and he calls Ancaeus
Happy for his wounds. With his last breath
He calls upon his aged father, his brothers,
His devoted sisters, his wife and, with a groan,
Perhaps his mother. The fire intensifies,
And with it the pain. Then both die down,
And fire and pain go out together.
As his spirit slips away into gentle air,
Grey ash slowly veils the glowing coals.   600

All of Calydon was devastated. Young and old
Lamented, noble and common both groaned.
The women of Calydon by Evenus' waters
Tore their hair and beat their breasts. The father
Lies on the ground and defiles his white hair
And aged head with dust, bitterly complaining
That he has lived too long; for the mother,

Seeing what she had done, has punished herself
With a dagger through her heart. Not if some god
Gave me a hundred speaking mouths, sheer genius,   610
And all Helicon has, could I ever capture
The lamentation of his wretched sisters.
Without a thought for decency they beat their breasts
Black and blue; caressed their brother's corpse,
While there was a corpse, and caressed it again;
Kissed the body and the bier where it stood;
Scooped up the ashes and pressed them to their breasts;
Threw themselves on his tomb, and clasping the stone
On which his name had been carved, drenched it with tears.
In the end Diana, satisfied with the destruction   620
Of the house of Parthaon, feathered their bodies—
All of them except Gorge and Deianeira—
Stretched out wings over the length of their arms
And gave them horny beaks, sending them forth
As Meleagrides, guinea hens, into the air.

★ ★ ★

Philemon and Baucis

*[The narrator, Lelex, is one of a number of heroes (including Theseus and
Pirithoüs) who are telling stories in the halls of the river god Acheloüs.
Pirithoüs has just expressed doubts as to the power of gods to bring about
transformations.]*

They were all shocked, and disapproved of such words,
Especially Lelex, mature in judgment and years,
Who said,
          "Immense is the power of heaven
And knows no end. Whatever the gods want   700
Is done, and, to boost your faltering faith,
There is an oak tree right next to a linden
Up in the Phrygian hills, ringed by a low wall.
I saw the spot myself when Pittheus

Sent me to the country his father once ruled.
There's a marsh close by, once habitable land
But now coots and other waterfowl live there.
Jupiter once went there disguised as a mortal,
And his son Mercury tagged along with him
But without his caduceus or winged sandals.   710
Looking for a place to rest, they knocked on
A thousand doors; a thousand doors stayed shut,
But one house did let them in, a little one
Thatched with straw and reeds from the marsh.
Pious old Baucis lived there with Philemon,
Who was the same age as his wife. The couple
Married in that cottage when they were young
And grew old there together. They made light
Of their poverty and so bore it easily.
There were no masters or servants. These two   720
Were the whole household, and the same people
Gave orders and obeyed. So, when the gods arrived
At this humble hearth and stooped to enter,
The old man set out a bench and told them
To sit down and relax, and Baucis bustled up
And threw on a rough coverlet. She scraped
The ashes from the fireplace and fanned
Yesterday's embers, feeding them with leaves
And dry bark and blowing them into flames
With her old woman's breath. Then she took down   730
Some split wood and dry twigs from the rafters,
Broke them up and put them under the bronze kettle.

Her husband had picked a cabbage from the garden,
And she chopped the leaves off from the stalk.
The old man had a forked stick and was fetching
A chine of smoked bacon that was hanging
From a blackened beam. Cutting off a little piece
Of this long-seasoned pork he put it in the pot
To boil with the cabbage. They passed the time talking,
And then put a long cushion stuffed with soft sedge   740
Onto a couch with a willow frame and legs.

They draped this with a cloth that they only used
On festal occasions, but even this was cheap
And worn with age. It went well with the couch.
The gods reclined. The old woman, skirts tucked up,
Put the table in place with trembling hands.
One of its legs was too short, so she propped it up
With a broken piece of tile. When she had it level
She wiped down the table with fresh mint
And set out some olives, both green and black,   750
Autumn cornel cherries pickled in wine lees,
Endive and radishes, cream cheese, and eggs
Lightly roasted in warm embers, all served
In earthenware dishes. After these appetizers
An embossed mixing bowl, no less silver
Than the rest of the ware, was put on the table
Along with beech-wood cups coated inside
With yellow wax. The steaming main course
Soon arrived from the hearth, and wine of no great age
Was served all around. Then a little space was made   760
For the dessert: nuts, wrinkled dried dates, plums,
And fragrant apples served in wide baskets
Along with purple grapes just picked from the vine.
A clear white honeycomb was set in the middle.
Besides all this, they brought to the table
Cheerful faces, high spirits, and abundant good will.

Meanwhile wine kept welling up in the mixing bowl
All by itself, so that as often as it was drained
It was never empty. Baucis and Philemon saw this
And didn't know what to think. They lifted   770
Their upturned hands and prayed, asking pardon
For the food they served and the poor accoutrements.
They had one goose, who guarded their little estate,
And were going to kill it for their divine guests.
But the goose was swift on the wing and wore out
The slow old people trying to catch it, dodging them
For a long time and finally taking refuge
With the gods themselves, who told them to let it live.

'We are gods,' they said. 'This wicked neighborhood
Will get its just deserts, but you will be spared.   780
Leave your house now and come along with us
Up the high mountainside.'
                                    The couple obeyed
And leaning on their staffs they struggled step by step
Up the long slope. When they were within a bowshot
Of the summit, they looked back and saw
Everything covered with water, except their house.
While they wondered at this, and wept for their friends,
The old house, which had been too small for two,
Turned into a temple. Forked poles became columns,
The thatch grew yellow and became a golden roof,   790
Figured gates appeared, and marble pavement
Covered the ground. Then Jupiter said calmly,

'And now, just old man, and woman worthy
Of your just husband, ask whatever you want.'

After he and Baucis had talked a little,
Philemon told the gods their joint decision:

'We ask to be your priests and your temple's caretakers,
And, since we've spent our lives together in harmony,
We ask to be taken the very same hour, so that I
May never see my wife's tomb, nor she bury me.'   800

Their prayer was answered. They took care of the temple
For the rest of their lives, until one day,
Old and worn out, they happened to be standing
In front of the sacred steps, talking about the place
And all that had happened there, when Philemon
Saw Baucis, and Baucis saw Philemon
Sprouting leaves. As the canopy grew
Over their faces, they cried out while they could
The same words together, 'Good-bye, my love,'
Just as the bark closed over their lips.   810
To this day the Bithynians who live there

Point out two trees growing close together
From a double trunk. These things were told to me
By sober old men with no reason to lie.
I certainly saw wreaths hanging from the branches
And when I put a fresh one there myself, I said,

'Whom the gods love are gods. Adore and be adored.'"

★ ★ ★

Book 9

★ ★ ★

Nessus and Deianeira

[The river god Acheloüs has just told the story of how he lost one of his horns in a wrestling match with Hercules for the hand of Deianeira.]

Acheloüs finished, and then one of the attendants,
A nymph with flowing hair and dressed like Diana,
Served them all from her plentiful horn, full
Of autumn's harvest, with apples for dessert.
Dawn came, and when the rising sun's first rays
Struck the mountain peaks, the young heroes left,   100
Not waiting for the floodwaters to subside
And the rivers to flow within their banks again.
Then Acheloüs hid his rustic face, and the scar
Where his horn once was, beneath his waters.
Still he had only the loss of his beautiful horn
To be sorry about. Otherwise he was fine,
And he could hide his loss with willow and reeds.
But you, Nessus, took an arrow through the back
Because of your passion for the same girl
And were utterly destroyed. It happened   110
When Hercules was going home with his bride
And had come to the swiftly flowing Evenus.
The water was higher than usual, swollen
With winter rains and swirling with eddies,
An impassable stream. As the hero stood there,
Afraid not for himself but for his bride,
Nessus came up, a strong Centaur who knew the fords.

"I'll get her to that other bank," he said. "With your strength
You can just swim across, Hercules."

And so,

Hercules entrusted Deianeira to Nessus.   120
She was trembling, afraid of the water
And of the Centaur. The hero, just as he was,
Still wearing his lion's skin and bearing his quiver
(He had tossed his club and bow to the opposite bank)
Jumped in, saying,

"All right, I'm in,

So much for this river."

And without bothering

To feel his way where the current ran smoothly
He made it across. He was just picking up his bow
When he heard his wife's voice. And he shouted
To Nessus, who was about to betray him,   130

"Where do you think you're going, you rapist?
I'm talking to you, Nessus, you half-breed! Don't even
Think about coming between me and mine!
If you're not afraid of me, remembering
Your father spinning on a wheel in Hell
Ought to be enough to stop you in your tracks.
I don't care how fast the horse half of you is;
If I can't run you down, I'll get you with my bow."

He made his last words come true, shooting an arrow
Straight into the back of the fleeing Centaur.   140
The barbed point stuck out from his chest. He tore it free,
And blood from both wounds came spurting out
Mixed with the venom of the Lernaean Hydra.
Saying to himself, "I will not die unavenged,"
Nessus gave Deianeira his tunic, still warm and wet
With poisoned blood, claiming it was a love charm.

The Death of Hercules

Time passed, and the deeds of great Hercules
Had filled the earth and appeased Juno's hate.

Fresh from a victory at Oechalia
He was preparing to fulfill his vows to Jove   150
At Cenaeum, when Rumor came ahead
Gossiping in your ears, Deianeira, Rumor,
Who loves to add the false to the true.
Small at first, she grows huge through lying,
And now she spread the tale that Hercules
Was enthralled with Iole. His loving wife
Believed the story and, devastated
With this report of her husband's new love,
She indulged her grief with a flood of tears.
But soon she said,

        "Why am I weeping?   160
My tears would make my rival glad. But since
She is on her way here, I need to make a plan
While I can, before another woman
Takes over my bed. Should I complain
Or grieve in silence? Go back to Calydon
Or, if I can't do more, stay here and oppose her?
O Meleager, what if I remember
That I am your sister and steel myself
To show what great evil a woman scorned
Is capable of—by slitting my rival's throat?"   170

She considered various courses of action
But in the end preferred to send her husband
The tunic soaked in Nessus' blood, hoping
That it would reinvigorate his failing love.
It was to Lichas that she brought the tunic
With no idea of the grief it would bring her.
With soft words the unhappy woman asked him
To take this present to her husband. The hero
Received the gift without knowing what it was
And clothed himself with the Hydra's poison.   180

He had just lit incense and was pouring wine
From a shallow bowl onto the marble altar.
The poison, released from the fabric by the heat,

Spread through Hercules' limbs. Hero that he was,
At first he held back his groans, but when the pain
Became unendurable, he pushed over the altar
And filled the woods of Oeta with his cries.
He tried to tear off the lethal tunic,
But it either stuck to his flesh, or, more horrible,
His skin came off with it, laying bare   190
His torn muscles and enormous bones. His blood
Seethed and hissed with the burning poison,
Like glowing hot metal plunged into water.
The insatiable heat dissolved his innards,
Black sweat flowed down his body, his sinews
Crackled and burned, and as his marrow melted
He stretched his hands to heaven and cried,

"Feast on my destruction, Saturnian Juno,
Feast! Look down from above on my affliction,
Cruel goddess, and glut your savage heart!   200
Or, even if I am your enemy, pity me,
Take away this hateful life, my tortured soul,
Born to suffer. Death will be a kindness
Fitting for a stepmother to bestow.
Was it for this that I overcame Busiris
Who defiled his temple with the blood of strangers?
That I hefted Antaeus the giant off the earth
Away from the strengthening touch of his mother?
That I did not fear Geryon's triple strength,
Or yours, Cerberus? That these hands of mine   210
Broke the strong bull's horn? That Elis knows
What these hands did, or the river Stymphalus,
The Parthenian woods, hands that brought back
The Amazon's belt chased with Scythian gold,
The golden apples guarded by the sleepless dragon?
For this that the centaurs could not withstand me,
Nor the boar that wasted Arcadia? That the Hydra
Couldn't win despite redoubling its heads?
What about when I saw the man-eating mares,
Their mangers full of mangled corpses, and killed   220

Both the horses and Diomedes, their master?
These arms strangled the Nemean lion; this neck
Held up the sky! Jupiter's savage wife
May be tired of imposing labors, but I
Am not tired of performing them. But now
A strange enemy is here, one that I cannot defeat
By courage or arms—a fire that eats my lungs
And all my body. But Eurystheus thrives!
How can anyone still believe in the gods?"

He spoke, and wounded to his heart's core,   230
Ranged along the steeps of Oeta, like a bull
Trailing a spear in its side, though the hunter
Has long since fled. You could see the great hero there,
Groaning, roaring in agony, trying again and again
To tear off his clothes, crashing down trees,
Filling the mountains with fury, stretching out his arms
To his father's sky.
                    Then he saw Lichas,
Cowering in fear on an overhanging cliff,
And all of his suffering came out as rage.

"You, Lichas," he cried, "didn't you bring me this gift?   240
Aren't you the cause of my death?"
                    Pale and trembling,
Lichas offered his timid excuses,
But while he was still speaking, still trying
To clasp the hero's knees, Hercules
Picked him up, and whirling him again and again
Over his head, flung him farther than a catapult could
Into the Euboean Sea. The man grew stiff and hard
As he hung in the air, and just as raindrops
Congeal in cold air and turn into snow
And then the snowflakes become solid hail,   250
So too Lichas, hurled from Hercules' hands
Through empty air, became bloodless with fear
And dried up into stone, the old story says.
And even today there is off the coast of Euboea

A low rock that preserves its old human form,
And, as if it could feel, sailors are afraid
To set foot on it, and they call this rock Lichas.

But you, Jupiter's illustrious son,
Cut down the trees on Oeta's steep slopes
And built a massive pyre. You told Philoctetes   260
To light the fire and take your bow, great quiver
And arrows, destined to see action in Troy again.
And as the flames began to lick the pyre's wood,
You spread the skin of the Nemean lion
On top, and with your club for a pillow, lay down
With a smile on your face, as if at a banquet
With wine flowing and a wreath on your head.
The crackling flames had enveloped the pyre
And reached the peaceful limbs of the hero,
Who scorned their strength. The gods were anxious   270
For the world's protector. Then Saturnian Jove,
Pleased with their sentiments, addressed them all:

"Your fear gladdens me, divine ones, and I rejoice
With all my heart that I am called lord and father
Of a grateful race of gods, and that my offspring
Enjoys the safety of your protective care,
And although he earned it by his prodigious deeds,
Still, I am obliged. But do not let your faithful hearts
Be filled with needless fear. Forget Oeta's flames!
He has conquered all and will conquer them too,   280
Feeling Vulcan's power only in the mortal half
His mother gave him. What he took from me
Is immortal, immune from fire and death,
And when it is done with earth I will receive him
On the shores of heaven. I trust that this
Will please all the gods, but if there is anyone
Who is sorry that Hercules will be a god,
Let him begrudge the prize, but he will also know
That it was deserved, and be obliged to approve."

The gods all assented; even Juno seemed pleased,   290
Although not perhaps with the last words of Jove,
Which annoyed her because they singled her out.
Meanwhile Mulciber had consumed what fire could,
And naught that could be recognized as Hercules
Now remained. Of his mother's contribution
Nothing was left, only traces of Jupiter.
And as a snake sloughs off age along with his skin
And luxuriates in new life, resplendent
In its fresh scales, so too when the Tiyrnthian
Sloughed off his mortal coils, his better part   300
Began to seem grander and more august,
And the Father Almighty drove his chariot
Down through the clouds to take him to heaven
And set him transfigured among the glittering stars.

★ ★ ★

Iphis and Ianthe

There lived near Phaestus,
And not far from the royal city of Cnossus,   770
A man named Ligdus, a freeborn citizen
Of humble birth and property to match,
Obscure otherwise, but blameless and true.
When the time was near for his wife to give birth,
He whispered in her ear these words of counsel:

"I pray for two things: that your delivery
Have the least possible pain, and that you give birth
To a baby boy. Girls are a much greater burden,
And it is their misfortune to be weak.
I hate to say it, but if you have a girl—   780
Heaven forgive me—it will have to be killed."

He said this, and their cheeks flowed with tears,
Both his wife's and his own. Telethusa

Kept begging her husband to change his mind
And not leave her with such little hope left,
But he would not relent. The hour had come
For the child to be born, and at midnight
Telethusa saw, or thought she saw in her dreams,
The goddess Isis standing before her bed
With a retinue of sacred beings. She wore   790
The horns of a crescent moon on her forehead
And was crowned with a golden garland of wheat.
The dog Anubis was with her, sacred Bubastis
With the head of a cat, the dappled bull Apis,
And the silent god with a finger on his lips.
The sacred rattles were there, and Osiris,
Forever sought for by Isis, and the serpent
Whose venom puts even the gods to sleep.
She seemed to be awake and see all this clearly
As Isis said to her,
                          "O Telethusa,   800
My devotee, you can stop worrying now
And forget about your husband's commands.
When Lucina has brought the child to light
Do not hesitate to raise it, be it girl or boy.
I am the goddess who helps my suppliants,
And you will never be able to complain
That you have worshipped an ungrateful goddess."

With these words, the deity left her room,
And the Cretan woman rose with joy from her bed,
Raising pure hands to the stars in earnest prayer   810
That the vision she had would prove to be true.

The pangs increased and at last she pushed her burden
Into the air and light. It was a girl,
But the father didn't know that, and the mother
Told the nurse, who was in on the lie,
To feed the boy. The father fulfilled his vows
And named the child after his grandfather,
Whose name had been Iphis. Telethusa thought

That this name was perfect. Its common gender
Meant it could be used without any deceit,   820
And so what began as a pious fraud
Remained undetected. The child wore boys' clothes,
And its face was beautiful whether it belonged
To a boy or a girl. Thirteen years went by,
And then, O my Iphis, your father arranged
A marriage for you with a girl named Ianthe,
Daughter of Cretan Telestes. She had golden hair
And all the women of Phaestus thought
She was the city's most beautiful girl. The two
Were matched in age and equally lovely.   830
They had gone to school together, and love
Touched their innocent hearts with equal longing
But not equal hope. Ianthe looked forward
To her wedding day, believing that Iphis,
Whom she thought was a man, would be her man.
But Iphis loved someone she never hoped to have,
And this in itself increased her passion,
A girl in love with a girl. She could barely
Hold back her tears.
                    "What will become of me,"
She said, "possessed by a strange and monstrous love   840
That no one has heard of? If the gods wanted
To spare me, they should really have spared me. If not,
And they really wanted to ruin me, at least
They should have given me some natural malady.
Heifers do not burn with love for heifers, nor mares
For mares. No, rams go for sheep, and does follow stags.
Birds mate like this too, and so do all animals:
No female desires another female.
I wish I'd never been born! Sure, Crete has produced
Every monstrosity, and Pasiphaë did make love   850
To a bull, but that was male and female. My passion
Is clearly even more insane. She had her bull
By being disguised as a heifer, and the male lover
Was the one taken in. But no ingenuity,
Not even if Daedalus himself flew back here

On his waxen wings, could change me from a girl
Into a boy. Or could he change you, Ianthe?

No, pull yourself together, Iphis, be strong,
And shrug off this useless and foolish love.
Look at what you were born, unless you want   860
To deceive yourself, and love what a woman should.
It is hope that begets love, and hope that feeds it.
And the facts of the matter deny you all hope.
No guardian keeps you from her dear embrace,
No jealous husband, no strict father, and she herself
Would not say no. But you still can't have her,
Can't be happy, even with all in your favor,
With men and all of the gods on your side.
None of my prayers have ever been denied;
The gods have given me all that they could.   870
She wants what I want, and both fathers approve,
But Nature won't allow it. Nature, more powerful
Than all of the gods, is working against me.
And now my long-awaited wedding has come,
And soon Ianthe will be mine—and not mine.
We'll be thirsty with water everywhere around.
Why would you, Juno, or you, Hymen, come
To a wedding with no groom but only two brides?"

She said no more. The other bride was burning
With equal passion, and prayed that you, Hymen,   880
Would come quickly.
                    Telethusa, meanwhile,
Fearing what Ianthe desired, put off the wedding
With a variety of excuses: pretended sickness,
Ominous visions. With no excuses left
And the postponed wedding only one day off,
She removed the sacred bands from her head
And from her daughter's, so that their hair hung loose,
And clinging to the altar, she prayed,
                    "O Isis,
Goddess of Paraetonium and the Mareotic fields,

Of Pharos and the seven mouths of the Nile,   890
Help us, I pray, and relieve our distress.
I saw you once, Goddess, you and your symbols
And knew them as I heard the bronze sistrum sound
And inscribed your commands on my mindful heart.
That my daughter here still looks on the light
And I have not been punished—this is your gift
And your counsel, Goddess. Pity us both
And lend us your aid."
                              Tears followed her words.
The goddess seemed to move, did move, her altar;
The temple doors shook, and the horns of the goddess   900
Shone like the moon as the bronze sistrum rattled.
Not yet carefree, but gladdened by this omen
Telethusa left the temple, followed by Iphis,
Whose stride was longer than before. Her complexion
Was now more tan than white, her features more chiseled,
Her hair now shorter and unadorned. There was more strength
In that frame than a girl would have, and in fact you were
No longer a girl, but a boy.
                              Go make offerings
At the temple, rejoice and be glad!
                              The two of them
Made offerings together, and in the temple   910
Set up a votive plaque with this inscription:

HIS VOWS AS A GIRL IPHIS FULFILLED AS A BOY.

The morning sun had unveiled the world,
When Venus appeared with Juno and Hymen,
And Iphis had his Ianthe at last.

Book 10

Orpheus and Eurydice

Trailing his saffron robes through the immense aether
Hymen flew down to the shores of the Cicones,
Heeding the vain summons of Orpheus' voice.
He was present, yes, but brought no solemn words,
No joyous expressions, no happy omen.
Even the torch that he held just hissed with teary smoke
And no matter how much he shook it, it would not catch fire.
The outcome was worse than the portent: the bride,
Walking through the grass with her naiad friends,
Was bitten in the heel by a snake and died.   10

When the Thracian bard had filled the upper air
With his laments, he made a bold descent
To the Taenarian Styx to try the spirits below,
And wading through the insubstantial images
Of the buried dead he came before Proserpina
And the lord of the unlovely realms of shades.
Touching the strings of his lyre, he sang,

"Rulers of the world beneath the earth,
To which all of us mortal creatures recede,
If you will permit me to speak the simple truth   20
Without a hint of lies, I have not come down here
To see lightless Tartarus, or to chain
The Medusan monster's three viperous throats.
I have come for my wife, bitten in the heel
By an adder whose poison has stolen her youth.
I wanted to be able to bear this, and I did try.
Love prevailed, a god known well in the world above
And perhaps, I think, even here below:
If the story of that old abduction is true,

Love joined you two as well.
                            By this place full of fear,   30
By immense Chaos and the silence of this vast realm,
Reweave, I beg you, Eurydice's hurried fates.
We are all owed to you, and after a brief delay
Sooner or later we all rush down to this place.
This is our destination, our last home, and you
Hold the longest reign over the human race.
She too, after she has lived a normal span of years,
Will be yours by right. We are asking for a loan.
But if the fates deny pardon for my wife,
I will not go back. Delight in the death of two."   40

As he said these things, plucking the strings
To his words, the bloodless shades wept. Tantalus
Stopped trying to scoop up the receding water,
And Ixion's wheel was stunned. The vultures
Left off from Tityus' liver, Belus' granddaughters
Put down their urns, and even you, Sisyphus,
Sat on your stone. Then for the first time, they say,
The Furies, charmed by his song, wet their cheeks,
Nor could the royal consort or her dark lord
Refuse his request. They called Eurydice,   50
Who was still among the recent shades,
Walking slowly with a limp from her wound.

Orpheus received her along with this condition:
He must not look back until he had left
The Valley of Avernus, or the gift would be void.
The path wound up through deafening silence
Along a steep, dark slope shrouded in fog.
They were approaching the upper rim when the lover,
Fearing for his partner and eager to see her,
Turned his eyes. She fell back at once,   60
Stretching out her arms, trying to catch and be caught,
And sorry to take hold of nothing but air.
Dying again, she did not blame her husband—
What could she complain of except she was loved?

She said her last good-bye, which he could barely hear,
And whirled back again to where she had been.

His wife had died twice now. Orpheus was as stunned
As that nameless man who saw Cerberus chained
And whose fear left him only when his nature did,
Cold granite numbing his entire body;   70
Or as Olenus, who willingly took on
The guilt of Lethaea, too proud of her beauty,
As the loving pair turned into a pair of stones
On watershed Ida. Orpheus yearned and prayed
To recross the Styx, but the ferryman refused.
For seven days he sat on the banks of the river,
Filthy and unfed, his only sustenance tears
And anguish of soul. Complaining that the gods
Of Erebus were cruel, he withdrew to the high,
Windswept steppes of Rhodope and Haemus.   80

The circling sun had three times returned
To watery Pisces, and Orpheus had rejected
All love of woman, whether because his love
Had turned out so badly, or he had pledged his faith.
Still, many women fell in love with the poet,
And many grieved when rebuffed. It was Orpheus
Who began the custom among Thracian men
Of giving their love to tender boys, and enjoying
That brief springtime of blossoming youth.

There was a hill, and on the hill a wide plain,   90
An area green with grass but without any shade.
When the poet born of the gods sat down there
And touched the resonant strings of his lyre,
Shade came to the place. Not a tree stayed away,
Not the Chaonian oak or the Heliades' poplars,
The high-crested chestnut, soft lindens and beech,
The virgin laurel, the brittle hazel, the tough ash
Used for spear shafts, many smooth-grained firs,
The ilex drooping with acorns, pleasant plane trees,

Colored maples, riverbank willows, watery lotus,   100
Evergreen boxwood and slender tamarisks,
Bicolor myrtles, and viburnum dark with berries.
You also came, tendriled ivies and grapes,
And elms cloaked in vines, mountain ash and pines,
Arbute trees loaded with ruby-red fruit,
The pliant palm, victory's prize, and the girded pine
With high crown, pleasing to the Mother of the Gods
Ever since Cybele's beloved Attis
Shed his human form and stiffened into its trunk.

★ ★ ★

Jupiter and Ganymede

The lord of heaven once burned with love
For Phrygian Ganymede, and found something
He preferred to be rather than what he was.
But not just any bird would do, only the eagle,
Who bore his thunderbolts. And so off he went
Through the world's air on lying wings and stole
The Trojan boy, who, against Juno's will,
Still serves cups of nectar to his Jupiter.

Apollo and Hyacinthus

And you, Hyacinthus, Phoebus would have placed   170
You in the sky, if grim Fate had given him time.
Still, you are eternal in your own way.
Every time spring pushes winter out
And Aries comes in after watery Pisces,
You come up and bloom in the emerald grass.
My father loved you above all others,
And Delphi, which is the navel of the earth,
Missed its master while the god was haunting
The banks of the Eurotas and unwalled Sparta.
He no longer honored the bow or the lyre   180
And, forgetful even of himself, was willing
To bear hunting nets, hold the dogs on leash,

Accompany you on the rough mountain ridges,
And with long intimacy feed his love's flame.

And now the Titan Sun was midway between
Night that was done and the still coming dusk,
When the two stripped down and, their skin gleaming
With rich olive oil, competed with the discus.
Phoebus swung it back, paused, and sent it flying
Off through the air to part the clouds with its weight.   190
It stayed aloft a long time before it fell to the ground,
A throw that exhibited both strength and skill.
The Spartan boy, incautious and caught up in the game,
Ran out to get the discus, but the hard earth
Kicked it back up and full into your face,
O Hyacinthus. The god turned as pale as the boy.
He picked up his limp form, tried to give him warmth,
Staunch his terrible wound, sustain his life with herbs.
But his arts were useless, the wound past curing.
Just as in a garden, if someone breaks the stems   200
Of violets or poppies or lilies, bristling
With their yellow stamens, they suddenly go limp
And droop, no longer able to stand upright,
Their heads bowed low, looking to the ground—
So too lies Hyacinthus' dying face. His neck,
Unable to sustain its own weight, falls back
On a shoulder. And Apollo said to him,

"You are fallen, cheated of the prime of youth,
And I see my guilt in your wound, O my sorrow
And my most grievous fault. My hand must be charged   210
With your destruction; I am the author of your death.
And yet what is my fault, unless playing with you
Can be called a fault, unless loving you
Can be called a fault? If only I could die with you
And give up my life! But since we are barred from this
By Fate's laws, you will always be with me,
And your name will ever be on my lips.
You will be the sound of my lyre, my songs

Will all be of you. And you will as a new flower
Imitate my groans with your petals' design.   220
And the time will come when a very great hero
Will be known by the name inscribed on this flower."

Apollo spoke the truth. The blood that spilled
On the ground, staining the grass, was no longer blood,
But a flower more brilliant than Tyrian dye,
Rising up like a lily except that its color
Was deep purple instead of silvery white.
Apollo was not done with this miraculous tribute
Until he inscribed the petals with his own groans—
AI AI—and the flower still bears these letters of grief.   230
Sparta, too, was proud that Hyacinthus was hers,
And his honor lasts to this day, a yearly celebration,
The ancestral festival of the boy Hyacinthus.

★ ★ ★

Pygmalion

*[Orpheus has just sung the story of the shameful behavior of the daughters
of Propoetus and their punishment. Orpheus continues here with the story
of Pygmalion.]*

Pygmalion had seen these women living in shame,
And, offended by the faults that nature had lavished
On the female psyche, lived as a bachelor
Without any bedmate. Meanwhile he sculpted
With marvelous skill a figure in ivory,   270
Giving it a beauty no woman could be born with,
And he fell in love with what he had made.
It had the face of real girl, a girl you would think
Who wanted to be aroused, if modesty permitted—
To such a degree does his art conceal art.
Pygmalion gazes in admiration, inhaling
Passion for a facsimile body.

He often touches the statue to find out whether
It is ivory or flesh, and is unwilling to admit
That it is ivory. He kisses it and thinks   280
His kisses are returned. He speaks to it,
And when he holds it he seems to feel
His fingers sinking into its limbs, and then fears
He might leave bruises where he has pressed.
He makes sweet talk to it, and brings it gifts,
The kind that girls like, shells and smooth pebbles,
Little birds and colorful flowers, and the Heliades'
Amber tears that drip down from trees. He drapes
Robes around it, puts jeweled rings on its fingers
And long necklaces around its décolletage.   290
All these things are beautiful, but the statue
Is no less beautiful nude. He lays it on a bed
Spread with coverlets dyed Tyrian blue and calls
The statue his bedmate, resting its reclining head
On downy pillows, as if it could feel them.

And now it was the festal day of Venus,
And all of Cyprus turned out to celebrate.
Heifers with gilded horns had fallen when the axe
Came down on their snowy necks, and incense
Smoked on the altars. Pygmalion offered   300
His sacrifice, and standing at the altar
Timidly prayed,
                    "O gods, if you can grant all things,
My prayer is that I may have as a wife,"
He didn't dare say, "my ivory girl,"
But said instead, "someone like my ivory girl."

But golden Venus, who of course was present
At her own festival, knew what his prayer meant,
And as an omen of her divinity's favor
The flame on the altar flared up three times.
Back home, he went to his simulacrum   310
And bending over the couch gave it a kiss.
She seemed to be warm. He kissed her again

And touched her breast with his hand. The ivory
Was growing soft to the touch, and as it lost
Its stiff hardness it yielded to his fingers,
As Hymettian wax softens under the sun
And can be kneaded and molded by the thumb
Into many forms, its use growing through use.
The lover is astounded. Cautiously rejoicing
And fearing he is mistaken, he tests his hopes   320
Again and again with his hand. It's a real body!
The veins were throbbing under his thumb.
Our Paphian hero poured out thanksgiving
To the goddess Venus, and pressed his lips
Onto real lips at last. The girl felt the kisses,
Blushed, and lifting her shy eyes up to the light
Took in the sky and her lover together.
The goddess attended the marriage she'd made,
And when nine moons had filled their crescent horns
A daughter was born to them, Paphos,   330
For whom the island of Paphos is named.

Myrrha and Cinyras

Her son was Cinyras; if he had been childless
He might have been counted among the fortunate.
My song is dire. Daughters, stay away; and fathers, too.
Or if my songs charm you, do not believe this story;
Believe instead that it never happened,
But if you do believe it, believe the punishment too.
And if nature allows a thing like this to be seen,
I congratulate this land on being far removed
From the regions that beget such iniquity.   340
Let the land of Panchaia be rich in balsam,
Let it bear cinnamon, costmary, and frankincense
Dripping from the trees, let it bear flowers galore,
Provided that it bears the myrrh tree too.
A new tree was not worth such a price as this.

Cupid swears that his weapons did not harm you
And absolves his torches of your crime, Myrrha.

One of the three Stygian sisters with a firebrand
And swollen vipers must have breathed on you.
It is a great offense to hate your father,   350
But love like this is a greater crime than hate.
You have your pick of the Orient's princes,
All of them vying to bed you in marriage.
Out of them all choose one man, Myrrha,
So long as a certain one is not among them.

She is aware of her despicable passion
And tries to resist it, saying to herself,

"What is my mind doing? What am I scheming?
O Gods, I pray, and Piety, and the sanctity
Of a parent, keep this sin from me and help me   360
To resist this crime—if indeed it is a crime.
But Piety refuses to condemn love like this.
Other animals mate without restriction,
And it is not shameful for a heifer to have
Her sire cover her, nor for a horse's offspring
To be his mate. A goat will go in among
Flocks he has fathered, and birds conceive
From birds who conceived them. Lucky them!
But humans have made malevolent laws,
And what Nature allows, their spiteful laws forbid.   370
Yet they say there are tribes where daughter and father,
Mother and son are joined, doubling natural affection.
It's just my bad luck not to have been born there.
Why do I keep thinking about things like that?
Forbidden hopes, begone! He's worthy to be loved,
But as a father. So, if I were not the daughter
Of great Cinyras, I could sleep with Cinyras,
But because now he is mine, he is not mine,
And my nearness is my loss. I'd be better off
As a stranger. I would leave my fatherland   380
To avoid this sin, but love keeps me from leaving,
Keeps me here so that I can be in Cinyras' presence,
See him, touch him, speak with him, kiss him,

If that's all I can do. But how could you hope for more,
You perverse creature? Do you have any idea
Of the names and relationships you are confusing?
Do you want to be your mother's rival
And your father's mistress? Your son's sister
And your brother's mother? And do you not fear
The sisters whose hair is bound with black snakes   390
And who shake their torches before the eyes
Of guilty souls? But since you have not yet sinned
With your body, don't conceive it in your heart
And pollute natural law with taboo fantasies.
Suppose you do want it; reality forbids it.
He's upright and moral, even old-fashioned—
And, oh, how I wish he had a passion like mine!"

Thus Myrrha. Cinyras, meanwhile, could not choose
Among the swarm of noble suitors his daughter had
And so went to her with their names and asked her   400
Whom she wanted as a husband. The girl was silent.
She stared into her father's face, and her eyes
Filled with warm tears. Cinyras took this to be
A virgin's shyness. He told her not to cry,
Wiped the tears from her cheeks and kissed her lips.
Myrrha was overjoyed, and when she was asked
What kind of husband she might want, she answered,
"Someone like you." Cinyras did not understand
What his daughter meant and praised her, saying,
"Stay this devoted." At the word "devoted,"   410
The girl looked down, conscious of her sin.

Midnight, and sleep had calmed human cares,
But Cinyras' daughter was awake all night,
Consumed by uncontrollable passion
And obsessed with her lust. Filled with despair
And then with resolve, flushing with shame
And then with desire, she does not know what to do.
As a tall tree that is being cut down,
All but the axe's last blow having fallen,

Wavers this way and that, threatening every side,   420
So too Myrrha, her mind and will weakened
By many blows, tottered this way and that
And tries to go in two directions at once.
She can find no rest from her passion but death,
And she decides on death. She rises, determined
To hang herself, and ties her sash from a rafter.
"Good-bye, dear Cinyras," she says, "and know
The reason for my death," as she fits the rope
Around her pale neck.

           They say her blurred words
Reached the ears of her nurse just outside her door.   430
The old woman went in and when she saw
The attempted suicide, she—all in the same moment—
Screamed, beat her breasts, tore her nightgown,
And unwound the rope from her darling's neck.
Then she had time to weep, hold her, and ask
The reason for the noose. The girl is mum
And keeps her eyes on the floor, regretting
That her halfhearted attempt to die was detected.
The old woman insists, bares her white hair
And depleted breasts, and begs by the girl's cradle   440
And first nourishment that she trust her nurse
With her grief's cause. The girl turns away groaning.
The nurse is determined to find out and promises
More than confidence.

           "Tell me," she says,
"And let me help you. I may be old
But I'm not a dolt. If it's some kind of madness
I have charms and herbs that will heal you.
If someone has put a spell on you, magic rites
Will dispel it. If the gods are angry with you,
They can be appeased with a sacrifice.   450
What else could it be? Your domestic affairs
Are safe and sound. Your mother and your father
Are alive and well."

           At the word "father"
Myrrha sighed from the bottom of her heart.

Even then the nurse had no idea
Of the girl's sinful thoughts, but she guessed
It was some love affair, and she kept pleading
For Myrrha to tell her, whatever it was.
The old woman held the weeping girl close
In her feeble arms and said to her,
                                        "I know,   460
You are in love. Now don't worry. In this affair
I will be completely devoted to you,
And your father will never know."
                                        The girl
Leapt madly from the old woman's bosom
And pressed her face into her bed, saying,

"Please, go away, or at least stop asking
Why I am so upset. It's horrible, sinful,
What you are trying so hard to know."

The old woman was shaken. Stretching out hands
That trembled with age and fear, she fell   470
At the feet of the girl she had nursed
And pleaded with her, now softly coaxing,
Now frightening her if she does not tell her secret.
She threatens to report her attempted suicide,
And she promises support if her love is confided.
The girl lifts her head and fills her nurse's bosom
With welling tears. She keeps trying to confess
But swallows her words and covers her shamed face
With her robes. Then she says,
                                        "O my mother,
Blessed in your husband."
                                        Just that, and she moans.   480
The nurse understood. Cold fear sank into her bones,
And the white hair stood stiffly on her head.
She said all that she could to drive this mad passion
Out of the girl, who understood how true
Her nurse's warnings were. Still, she was resolved
To die if she could not obtain her desire.

"Live then," said the nurse. "You will have your—"
She did not dare say "father." She said no more,
Except to confirm her promise with an oath.

Ceres' yearly festival was being celebrated   490
By pious married women. Clothed in pure white,
They brought garlands of wheat as first offerings,
And for nine nights abstained from love, or even
The touch of a man. Cenchreis, the king's wife,
Was among them, observing the secret rites.
The king's bed being void of a legitimate wife,
The nurse, attentive but with bad intentions,
Told Cinyras, whom she found had drunk too much,
Of a spectacular beauty (she gave a false name)
Who was in love with him. When he asked the girl's age,   500
She said, "The same as Myrrha." Told to go get her,
She cried out as soon as she got home,
                                        "Rejoice,
My child. We've won!"
                            The unhappy girl
Did not feel joy with all her heart, but felt
Sad presentiments. Still, she was glad too,
So discordant were the feelings she had.

It was the hour when all is hushed,
And between the Bears Boötes has turned
The pole of his wagon down to the horizon.
Myrrha came to her evil deed. The golden moon   510
Fled from the sky; the stars hid behind black clouds
And deprived the night of its fiery sparks.
You were the first, Icarius, to cover your face;
And you, Erigone, his daughter, translated
To the stars for your pious love of your father.
Three times Myrrha stumbled, an omen
Calling her back. Three times the eerie cry
Of the funereal owl served as a portent,
But still she went on, her shame diminished
By the shadows of night. With her left hand   520

She clutches her nurse, and with the other
She gropes her dark way. Now she has reached
The chamber's threshold and is opening the door,
Now she is led within, but her knees buckle,
She is pale and bloodless, and there is no life
In her limbs as she moves. The nearer she gets
To her abomination, the more she shudders at it,
Regrets her boldness, and wishes she could go back
Unrecognized. The nurse leads her by the hand
Up to the high bed and delivers her,   530
Saying, "Take her, Cinyras, she is yours,"
As she joins them together in unholy love.
The father receives his own flesh in his bed
And tries to calm down the frightened girl,
Encouraging her and calling her "Baby,"
Just as at some point she calls him "Daddy,"
So that names would play a part in their sin.

She went from the chamber full of her father,
Carrying in her womb desecrated seed
And a maculate conception. The next night   540
Doubled their sin, nor was it the last.
Finally, after so many beddings, Cinyras,
Eager to know what his mistress looked like,
Brought in a lamp and saw his crime and his daughter.
Speechless with grief, he unsheathed his bright sword,
And Myrrha escaped death only by fleeing
Into the shadows of night. She made her way
Through the back country, leaving Arabia's palms
And the fields of Panchaia. Utterly weary
After nine months of wandering, she finally rested   550
In the Sabaean land, now hardly able to bear
The burden of her womb. Perplexed,
Caught between fear of death and weariness of life,
She embraced this prayer:
                              "If there is any god
Open to my prayers, I do not refuse
The punishment I deserve. But to avoid

Offending the living by my life or the dead
By my death, exclude me from both realms.
Transform me, and deny me both life and death."

Some god answered her final prayer. The earth   560
Closed over her legs as she spoke, and roots
Popped out of her toes to support the high trunk.
Her bones became sturdier, and while the marrow
Remained much the same, her blood became sap,
Her arms became branches, her fingers became twigs,
And her skin hardened to bark. The growing tree
Had now bound her heavy womb, buried her breast,
And almost covered her neck; but she could not wait,
And sank her face down into the rising wood,
Plunging it into bark. And although she has lost   570
Her old senses and feelings along with her body,
She still weeps, and the warm drops flow down the tree.
Even her tears are honored, and the myrrh
That drips from the bark preserves its mistress' name,
Which will be spoken through all the ages.

Meanwhile, the misbegotten baby had grown
Inside the tree and was now trying to find a way
To leave its mother and come into the world.
The pregnant tree swells in its midsection
And the pressure strains the mother. The pangs   580
Cannot be voiced, nor can Lucina be called
In the voice of a woman in labor. But like one,
The tree bends, groans, and is wet with falling tears,
And gentle Lucina stood near the moaning branches,
Laid on her hands, and chanted childbearing spells.
The tree cracked open and through its split bark
Delivered a baby boy. The naiads nestled
The wailing infant in leaves and anointed him
With his mother's tears. Even Envy would praise
The boy's beauty, for he looked like one   590
Of the naked Cupids you see in paintings.
Either give him a light quiver or take theirs away
And you wouldn't be able to tell them apart.

Venus and Adonis

Time glides by and slips away from us
Before we know it; nothing is swifter than years.
The son of both his sister and grandfather,
Lately concealed in a tree and lately born,
Then a most beautiful baby boy, then a youth,
Now a young man and even more beautiful.
He arouses Venus herself, and so avenges   600
His mother's passion. It happened this way.
While the goddess' son, quiver on his shoulder,
Was kissing his mother he accidentally
Grazed her breast with a protruding arrow.
The wounded goddess pushed her son away,
But the scratch was deeper than it looked.
Before she knew it she was deeply in love
With a beautiful man. She cared no more
For the shores of Cythera, forgot about Paphos
Ringed by the deep sea, and about Cnidos   610
With all its fish, and Amathus with its copper mines.
She even stayed away from heaven. Adonis
Is more appealing than heaven. She has him
And holds him, is his companion, and although
She is used to her beauty rest in the shade,
Now she tucks up her robes just like Diana
And ranges over the mountain ridges,
Over rocks and thorns, urging on the hounds
In pursuit of animals that are safe to hunt,
Headlong hares or stags with branching antlers   620
Or timid does, avoiding ravenous wolves
And things with claws, like bears, and lions
All bloody with the slaughter of cattle.
And she warns you too, Adonis, for what it's worth,
To fear these beasts.
          "Be brave," she said,
"With prey that runs away; boldness isn't safe
With bold animals. Do not be rash, dearest boy,
At my expense; and don't challenge those beasts
That nature has armed, or your glory may come

At great cost to me. Neither youth nor beauty,   630
Nor anything that has moved the goddess Venus,
Moves bristling boars and lions, or touches the minds
Of things in the wild. A boar's curving tusks
Strike like lightning, and a lion's angry charge
Is just as bad. I hate animals like that."

When he asks her why, she says,
                              "I'll tell you why,
And you will be amazed at an ancient monstrosity.
But I'm tired from all this unaccustomed effort,
And, look, there's a poplar with inviting shade,
And turf for a couch. I'd love to lie here with you"   640
(And down she lay), "on the ground."
                                     She rested
Both on the grass and on him, cushioning her head
On his chest, and interspersing words and kisses,
Told him the tale of Atalanta and Hippomenes.

Atalanta and Hippomenes

"You may have heard of a girl who used to beat men,
Fast men, in a footrace. That wasn't just a story:
She really did beat them. And you couldn't say
Whether her speed or beauty deserved more praise.
Now when she asked the oracle about a husband
The god responded,
                           'You don't need a husband,   650
Atalanta. Run away from all husbands. And yet,
You will not run away, and will lose yourself living.'

The god's oracle terrified the girl, and she lived
In the shady woods unwedded, and repelled
Her insistent suitors with a harsh condition.

'I am not to be won,' she said, 'until I lose a race.
Line up and run against me. A wife in bed
Will go to the swift; the slow pay with their death.
Those are the rules.'
                        She was pitiless alright,

But her beauty was so overwhelming that even   660
On this condition, a crowd of rash men lined up.
Hippomenes had taken a seat to watch
This travesty of a race and had asked,
'Who would take a risk like this just to get a wife?'
And he condemned the young men's undue love.
Then he saw her face and unclothed body,
Beauty such as mine, or yours, if you were a woman.
He was amazed, and stretching out his hands,

'Forgive me,' he said, 'for blaming you just now.
I had no idea of the prize in this contest!'   670

As he praises her he conceives a passion,
And, jealous and fearful, hopes that none of the youths
Will win the race.
            'But why don't I take a chance
And give it a try?' he asks. 'God helps the bold.'

While Hippomenes was thinking it over,
The girl flew by with wings on her feet.
Though she seemed as fast as a Scythian arrow,
It was her beauty that he admired more,
And her running itself creates its own beauty.
Her sandals' feathers swoosh in the breeze,   680
Her hair floats back from her ivory shoulders,
Embroidered ribbons flutter at her knees,
And her girlish body flushes with pink
The way a marble courtyard is stained with light
That is filtered through a purple awning.
While the stranger observed all this, the finish line
Was crossed. Atalanta took the winner's wreath,
And the losers groaned and paid the penalty.

Hippomenes, undeterred by what happened to them,
Stepped forward and looked the girl in the eye   690
As he said,
            'Why are you going for easy victories
Over slugs like this? Come on and race against me.

If I happen to win, there's no shame in you losing
To someone like me. Megaerus of Onchestus
Is my father and his grandfather is Neptune,
So I am the great-grandson of the Lord of Sea.
And my own prowess matches my pedigree.
Then again, if I lose, you will have the glory
Of having defeated Hippomenes.'

As he said these things, the daughter of Schoenus   700
Had a soft look on her face and couldn't decide
Which she wanted, to be conquered or conquer.
She said to herself,
                          'Some god must not like
Beautiful boys and wants to destroy this one
By making him risk his life so he can marry me.
In my opinion, I am not worth the price.
It's not just his good looks, although I like his looks,
But the fact that he really is still just a boy.
It's not he himself, but his youth that moves me.
And then there's his courage, his fearlessness   710
In the face of death. And let's not forget
That he's four generations removed from Neptune.
And that he loves me, and thinks marrying me
Is worth so much that he's willing to die
If cruel Fortune denies me to him.
Leave while you can, stranger! Run far away
From this bloody wedlock. Trying to marry me
Is a deadly affair. No girl would refuse you;
You could easily be wed to a girl with good sense.
But why do I care about you so much   720
When so many others have already died?
He can take care of himself! And he can die, too,
Since he didn't take the warning of the others' deaths
And doesn't value his life. But will he be killed
Because he wanted to live with me? Undergo
Undeserved death as the penalty for love?
My victory will mean unbearable hatred for me.
But it's not my fault. Oh, please, just withdraw!

Or since you're so crazy, I hope you run faster.
Oh, look how young and girlish he looks. Ah,   730
Poor Hippomenes, I wish you'd never looked on me.
You were so worthy of life. If I were happier,
If the cruel Fates did not deny me marriage,
You were the only one I would have in my bed.'

Now her father and the crowd were calling out
For the usual race, when Hippomenes
Called upon me:
                     'Cytherea, help my daring,
And encourage the fire of love that you've lit!'

A kindly breeze brought me this very nice prayer,
And it touched my heart, but there wasn't much time.   740
There's a field called Tamasus, the richest soil
In all of Cyprus, and from ancient times
Dedicated as one of my sacred precincts.
In the middle of the field is a gleaming tree
With rustling gold leaves and golden branches.
I had just been there and happened to have
Three golden apples I had picked in my hands.
I approached Hippomenes, showing myself
Only to him, and told him how to use them.

The trumpets blared and the runners were off,   750
Skimming the sand with flying feet. You would think
They could run on waves without wetting their soles
Or graze ears of ripe grain standing high in a field.
The boy's spirits were buoyed by encouraging shouts,

'Go, Hippomenes, turn on your sprint!
Give it all you've got. You've got her now!'

But who knows whether Megaerus' heroic son
Or Schoenus' daughter was more pleased with these words?
There were many times she could have passed him
But lingered a while to look at his face   760

Before reluctantly leaving him behind.
He was panting hard, and the finish line
Was still far off when he lobbed the first apple.
She was astonished and veered off course
To pick up the spinning gold. Hippomenes
Was pulling ahead and the spectators cheered,
But she made up the ground and passed him again.
She delayed to go after the second apple,
Then surged once more. They were coming down the stretch
When he prayed, 'Be with me now, Goddess,   770
Who gave me this gift,' and threw the shining apple
Hard and sideways into the field. It would take longer
For her to get it back, and the girl hesitated.
But I made her go get it and made the fruit heavier,
Slowing her down with both the detour and weight.
But my story is getting longer than the race itself.
The virgin was passed; the winner led away his prize.

Venus and Adonis (continued)

Now, Adonis, did I deserve to be thanked,
Have incense offered? He didn't think to thank me
Or offer me incense. I was hurt by his contempt   780
And flew into a rage. To forestall future slights
I decided to make an example of them both.

They were passing a temple deep in the woods,
A temple of Cybele, the Mother of the Gods.
Great Echion had built it in days gone by,
Fulfilling a vow. They had journeyed far
And wanted to rest. My divine power
Instilled in Hippomenes an untimely desire
To make love. There was a dim, shallow cave
Close to the temple, roofed with natural pumice,   790
A sanctuary of the old religion, where priests
Had installed wooden figures of the ancient gods.
They went in and desecrated that holy place
With forbidden intercourse. The sacred images
Averted their gaze, and the Great Mother,

With her turreted crown, was about to plunge
The guilty couple into the waters of Styx,
But the punishment did not seem severe enough.
Instead, tawny manes covered their once smooth necks,
Their fingers curved into claws, their arms changed to legs,   800
Their weight shifted to their chests, and they swept
The sandy ground with tails. Their faces were angry,
Their words were growls. Instead of bedrooms
They now haunt the wilds. Terrifying to others,
Their teeth champ the bit of Cybele as lions.
These and all other wild beasts like them
That don't run away but attack head on,
Please, my dearest, for my sake, avoid,
Or your manly courage might undo us both."

With that warning the goddess made her way   810
Through the air, drawn by her swans. But the boy
Felt himself too much a man to take such advice.
His hounds were soon on the trail of a boar
And rousted it from its hiding place. As it charged
Out of the woods Cinyras' young grandson
Got his spear into him with an angled thrust,
But the enraged animal used his curved snout
To root out the spear, drenched with his blood,
And went after the boy, who was panicking now
And running for his life. The boar sank his tusks   820
Deep into his groin and left Adonis to die
On the yellow sand. The Cytherean,
Her light car pulled through the air by flying swans,
Had not yet reached Cyprus when she heard the groans
Of the dying boy far off in the distance
And turned her white swans. When she saw him from the air,
His life ebbing away with his blood, she leaped down,
Tore her garments and hair, and beat her breast
With hands not suited to such lamentation.
And remonstrating with the Fates,

                      "But not all,"   830
She said, "will be yours to decide. My grief,

Adonis, shall be memorialized, and every year
Your death and my grief will be reenacted
In ritual. But your blood will be transmuted
Into a flower. If Proserpina once
Could change the nymph Menthe into fragrant mint,
Shall I be begrudged the transformation
Of Cinyras' heroic grandson, Adonis?"

And she sprinkled the blood with aromatic nectar.
Imbued with this essence, the blood swelled up
Like a clear bubble that rises from yellow mud,
And within an hour up sprang a flower
The color of blood, like a pomegranate bloom.
But its enjoyment is brief, for it does not cling
To its stem but easily falls when shaken
By the winds for which the anemone is named.

Book 11

The Death of Orpheus

While the poet from Thrace was enthralling trees,
Wild beasts and even stones that followed him,
The Ciconian women, animal skins draping
Their raving breasts, saw Orpheus from a hilltop
Arranging a song to the chords of his lyre,
And one of them, hair floating in the breeze, said,
"There he is, the man who scorns us!" and hurled
Her spear at the Apollonian singer's mouth,
But the shaft sprouted leaves and only grazed him.
The next missile was a stone. Stopped in midair   10
By the sound of voice and lyre, it fell at his feet
As if begging forgiveness for its audacity.
But the assault escalated without restraint,
And mad Fury ruled. Everything they threw
Would have been mollified by his music,
But the enormous clamor of Berycyntian flutes,
Of drums and breast-beating and Bacchic ululation,
Drowned out the lyre's sound. The stones finally grew red
With the blood of the poet, unheard in the end.

The Maenads first tore apart the innumerable birds,   20
The snakes, the animals still entranced by his voice,
And so stole the glory of Orpheus' triumph.
Then they turned on the singer with bloody hands,
Gathering like birds when they spot a night owl
Wandering in the daylight; and he is like a deer
In an amphitheater, soon to perish on the morning sand
As the dogs close in. They rushed at the poet, hurling
Their green-leaved thyrsi, made not for this use.
Some threw clods of earth, some branches ripped from trees,
Some stones. But more substantial weapons were at hand.   30

It happened that yokes of oxen were plowing the soil,
And, nearby, sturdy peasants were digging up fields,
Their arms glistening with sweat. When they saw
The advancing women, they ran, leaving behind
The tools of their trade. Scattered through the empty fields
Lay grub hoes, heavy pick-axes, long mattocks;
The savage women made off with these, and after
Tearing apart the oxen threatening them with their horns,
They rushed back to attend to the fate of the poet,
And as he stretched out his hands, speaking for the first time   40
To no effect and moving them not a bit with his voice,
The sacrilegious women undid him, and—O God—
Through that mouth, heard by rocks and understood by beasts,
His soul was exhaled and drifted off in the air.

The mourning birds wept for you, Orpheus,
The throngs of animals, the flinty rocks,
And the woods that had so often followed your songs,
The trees shedding their leaves as they grieved for you
With heads shorn. They say that rivers were swollen
With their own tears, and that nymphs of wood and stream   50
Wore black and grey and kept their hair disheveled.
His limbs lay all over the fields, but his head and lyre
Were received by you, O Hebrus, and as they floated
Downstream, his lyre—it was a miracle—
Played mournful notes, and his lifeless tongue
Murmured mournfully, and mournfully the banks replied.
And now, borne onto the sea, they left their native stream
And came ashore near Methymna on Lesbos.
As the severed head lay on that foreign beach,
Its hair still dripping with the spume of the sea,   60
A serpent attacked it. But Apollo appeared
And fended the serpent off in midstrike, turning
Its wide open jaws, just as they were, into stone.

The poet's shade went beneath the earth,
And all that he had seen before he recognized now.
Searching through the Fields of the Blessed

He found Eurydice and caught her up
In his eager arms. Now they walk together,
Matching steps. Sometimes she is in front,
Sometimes he takes the lead, and Orpheus
Can always look back at his Eurydice.

But Bacchus saw that this crime was avenged.
Grieved at the loss of his sacred poet,
He bound all of those Thracian women
Who witnessed the outrage with twisted roots.
The path that each of them took through the woods
Would tug at her toes and jam their tips
Into the solid earth. It was just like a bird
Who has got its leg caught in a snare
A cunning fowler has set; it flaps its wings,   80
And by its struggles draws the noose tighter.
So too these women, fixed in the clinging soil,
Desperately tried to break free, but the tough roots
Held them in place no matter their struggles.
And when they looked to see where their toes were,
Their feet, their nails, they saw the wood
Creep up their shapely legs. When they tried
To smack their thighs with grieving hands
They hit hard oak. Their breasts too became oak,
And oaken their shoulders. You would think their arms   90
Had become real branches, and you would not be wrong.

Midas

But not even this was enough for Bacchus.
He left those fields with a worthier retinue
And made for the vineyards near his own waters,
The Timolus River and the Pactolus,
Although the latter was not yet a golden stream
Envied for its precious sand. His usual crew,
Satyrs and Bacchants, were with him in droves,
But Silenus was not there. Some Phrygian peasants
Had captured him while he was stumbling along   100
Under the influence of old age and wine.

hey bound him with wreaths and led him to Midas,
Their king, whom Thracian Orpheus had taught,
Along with Eumolpus, the rituals of Bacchus.
When Midas saw it was his old companion
In the Bacchic orgies, he held a festival
To celebrate his honored guest's arrival,
And they feasted nonstop for ten days and nights.
When the eleventh dawn banished the ranking stars
The king rode merrily to the Lydian fields   110
And gave Silenus back to the youthful god
Who once was his ward. Bacchus was happy
To have his foster father back and as a reward
Granted Midas whatever he wanted,
A pleasing gift but not one that the king
Would use at all well.
                              "Grant," he said
That whatever I touch will turn to gold."

The god nodded and gave him the harm he asked for,
Sorry he hadn't seen fit to request something better.

Our hero went off pleased with his fatal gift   120
And tried it by touching things one at a time.
Not really believing, he broke off a green twig
From a hanging oak branch. The twig became gold.
He picked up a stone, and it blanched into gold.
He touched a clod of earth, and at his potent touch
It became a lump of gold. He plucked some ripe
Ears of wheat. It was a golden harvest.
He picked an apple from a tree. You would think
That it came from the garden of the Hesperides.
If he brushed his fingers on the soaring columns   130
The columns gleamed. When he washed his hands,
The water could delude a Danaë. His mind
Could hardly contain his hopes, imagining
That everything was gold. Deliriously happy,
He sat down at a table on which his servants
Had set out an elaborate feast, but when he picked up

A piece of bread, the bounty of Ceres
Became stiff and hard in his hand. If he tried to bite
Any piece of food, his teeth only closed on
A hard layer of gold. Water mingled with wine,   140
The wine of Bacchus who gave him his gift,
Flowed into his mouth as molten gold.

This was an alarming turn of events. Rich
And yet wretched, he yearns to flee his wealth,
And he hates what he asked for. No amount of food
Can relieve his hunger. His throat burns with thirst,
And he is, through his own fault, tortured by gold.
Lifting his hands and glistening arms to heaven,
He cried,
            "Forgive me, Father Lenaeus,
For I have sinned. Have mercy upon me,   150
And save me from this glittering curse!"

The gods are kind. Because he confessed his sin,
Bacchus restored him to what he was before
And rescinded the pledged gift. And he said,

"So you will not remain circumscribed by gold
That you so foolishly desired, go to the river
That laps great Sardis and work your way upstream
Against the current until you come to its source.
There you must submerge your head and body
In the gushing water, and so wash away your guilt."   160

Midas went to the water and did as directed,
And the golden touch suffused the whole river,
Passing from the man's body into the stream.
And even today the river's ancient vein
Still seeds the bordering fields with gold,
Their moistened soil turning hard and yellow.

Midas now despised wealth and lived in the woods
And fields, worshipping Pan, whose haunts

Are caves in the hills. But he remained dull-witted
And his mind would be his worst enemy once more.   170
Tmolus, a high peak, looks out over the sea,
One steep slope extending down to Sardis,
The other down to little Hypaepae, where Pan,
Impressing some young nymphs with his music,
Played gentle airs on his wax-joined reed pipe.
He went too far when he slighted Apollo's songs
In comparison with his own and wound up
Outmatched in a contest judged by Tmolus.

The old judge sat on his own mountain top
And shook his ears free from the trees. He wore   180
Only an oak wreath on his dark blue hair,
And acorns hung around his hollow temples,
Looking at the pastoral deity he said,
"There is no delay on the part of the judge."
Then Pan began to play on his rustic pipes
And the foreign melody charmed Midas' ears
(He happened to be nearby). When Pan was done,
Venerable Tmolus turned his face toward Phoebus,
And his whole forest turned with his face.
Phoebus Apollo's golden head was wreathed   190
With laurel from Parnassus, and his mantle,
Dyed deep Tyrian purple, swept the ground.
In his left hand was his lyre, inlaid with gems
And Indian ivory, and his plectrum
Was in his right. His very pose was an artist's.
When his trained thumb swept the strings, the sweet music
So charmed Tmolus that he ordered Pan
To lower his reeds before the lyre.

The holy mountain's verdict pleased everyone
Except for Midas, who called it unjust.   200
Apollo did not allow ears so insensitive
To keep their human form. He stretched them out
And covered them with coarse grey hair,
Great floppy things with the power to move.

Human otherwise, he now had the one deficit
Of wearing the ears of a slow-moving ass.
Desperate for a disguise, he tried to soften
The shame of his temples with a purple turban,
But the slave who cut his hair saw his disgrace.
He did not dare reveal it, but could not keep quiet,   210
And so he went off and dug a hole in the ground
And whispered into the excavation
What kind of ears he had seen on his master.
Then he filled the hole up, burying there
His testimony, and then went quietly home.
But a thick stand of reeds began to grow there
And when they reached full size at the end of the year,
They betrayed the digger, for, stirred by a breeze,
The reeds repeated the words he had buried
And revealed the truth about his master's ears.   220

★ ★ ★

[No selections from Book 12 are included.]

Book 13

★ ★ ★

Polydorus and Polyxena

Across from Troy is the land of the Bistones,
Where Polymestor had his royal court.
This was where Priam sent his son Polydorus,
To be reared in secret away from the war,
A wise plan if Priam had not sent with him   520
A treasure large enough to reward criminality
And tempt the greedy. When Troy's fortunes waned,
Polymestor slit his foster child's throat
And threw the body from a cliff into the sea,
As if murder and corpse could be jointly disposed of.

It was on this Thracian coast that Agamemnon
Moored his fleet to wait out a storm. Suddenly,
The earth split open and the ghost of Achilles
Rose up, as large as life and looking just as he did
On the day when he threatened Agamemnon,   530
Unjustly pulling his sword on the king.

"So, you are leaving, Achaeans," he cried out,
"Forgetting me; your gratitude for my courage
Is buried with me. Do not do this! Honor
My tomb by sacrificing Polyxena
And so appease the shade of Achilles."

His old comrades obeyed the pitiless ghost.
Polyxena, her mother's sole consolation,
Was torn from her arms, an ill-fated girl
Braver than any grown woman. She was led   540

To Achilles' funeral mound, there to become
A sacrificial victim. She never forgot
Who she was, even when she was placed
Before the grim altar and understood
That the savage rites were being prepared for her.
When she saw Neoptolemus standing there
And staring at her with sword in hand, she said,

"Avail yourself of my noble blood. Go ahead,
No need to wait. Just sink your sword deep
Into my throat or my breast." And she bared   550
Her throat and her breast. "Polyxena
Will not be a slave to any man, nor will you
Placate any god with a rite such as this.
I only wish that my mother not know of my death;
My mother diminishes my joy in death,
But my death should not be as dreadful to her
As her own life. All I ask, if my request is just,
Is that you move away, so that I may go freely
To the Stygian shades. Do not let a man's hands
Touch my virgin flesh. My blood pure and free   560
Will be more acceptable to whoever it is
You are trying to appease by slaughtering me.
And if my last words still move any of you
(The daughter of Priam, no captive asks you),
Return my body to my mother unransomed.
Let her pay with tears, not gold, for the sad right
Of burying me. She paid with gold when she could."

She spoke, and the people could not restrain
Their tears, as she could hers. The priest too wept
And driving the sword in against his will   570
Pierced her proffered breast. Her knees buckled,
And as she sank to the earth she kept to the end
Her look of fearless courage, taking care
Even as she fell to keep herself covered
And guard the honor of her chastity.

Hecuba

The Trojan women gathered her up
And counted how many children of Priam
There were to lament. And they wept for you also,
Hecuba, who just yesterday were called
The queen consort, the royal mother, 580
The very image of a flourishing Asia.
But now you are wretched even for a captive,
Unwanted by victorious Ulysses
Except that you had given birth to Hector,
Who never imagined such a lord for his mother.
Now, embracing the body left empty
Of that brave spirit, she bestows upon it
The tears she has shed so often for her country,
Her sons, and for her husband, pouring them
Into her daughter's wound, covering her lips 590
With kisses, and beating again her bruised breasts.
Then, sweeping her white hair in the congealed blood,
She uttered these words and more from her torn breast:

"My child, the last cause for your mother to grieve—
For what else is left?—here you lie, and I see your wound,
My wound, which you have so I would not lose
Even one of my children without any bloodshed.
Because you were a woman I thought that you
Would be safe from the sword, but you, a woman,
Have died by the sword, and the same Achilles 600
Who has destroyed Troy and made me childless,
Killing so many of your brothers, has now killed you.
When he fell to Paris' and Apollo's arrows,
I said that Achilles need no longer be feared,
But I still have to fear him. Although he is buried,
His very ashes rage against our race,
We feel him as an enemy even in his tomb.
I have borne my children for Aeacus' grandson!
Great Troy has fallen; our nation has come
To an awful end. But it did come to an end. 610

For me alone Ilium still survives,
And my troubles go on. Not long ago
I had everything, so many sons and daughters
And their husbands and wives, and my husband.
Now I am exiled, ragged, torn from the graves
Of my loved ones, dragged off to be a prize
For Penelope. She will point me out
To the Ithacan women as I spin her wool
And say, 'That is the famous mother of Hector,
Priam's queen.' Now you, my Polyxena,   620
The only one left, after so many were lost,
To comfort my grief, you have been sacrificed
On an enemy tomb, and I have given birth
To a funeral offering for the enemy dead.
Why should I go on living, numb with sorrow,
Why cling to life, preserved in wrinkled old age?
Why cruel gods, prolong an old woman's life,
Unless to see more funerals? Who would think
That Priam could be happy when Ilium fell?
In death he is happy. He does not see you dead,   630
My daughter, and he left his life and his kingdom
At the same time. What a splendid funeral
You will have, a royal maiden buried
In her ancestral tomb! This is no longer
The fortune of our house. Your funeral offerings
Will be your mother's tears, and a handful
Of foreign sand. I have lost everything,
But I still have some reason to live, to endure
A little while longer: his mother's dearest
And now only child, once my youngest son,   640
My Polydorus, sent to the Thracian king
Who rules these shores. But why do I delay
To cleanse your wound and wash your face of blood?"

Hecuba spoke, and the old woman stumbled
Down to the shore, tearing her white hair as she went.
"Give me an urn, Trojan women," she said,
Intending to draw some water from the sea.

There she saw the body of Polydorus
Cast up on the shore, rent with gaping wounds
By Thracian weapons. The Trojan women   650
Cried aloud, but Hecuba was dumb with a grief
That blocked not only her voice but her rising tears.
She stood like a stone, her eyes fixed
Sometimes on the ground, sometimes lifted
In horror to the sky, and at times resting
On the face of her son and upon his wounds.
And as she looked more and more at his wounds
Her rage became lethal, finally blazing forth
As if she were still the queen, bent on vengeance
And wholly absorbed in thoughts of punishment.   660
And just as a lioness who has had her suckling cub
Stolen from her and tracks down her unseen enemy
In silent fury, so too Hecuba, mingling grief
With wrath, forgetting her years but not her spite,
Went straight to Polymestor, the murder's architect,
And got an audience with him, pretending she had
A hoard of gold to reveal, as a bequest to her son.
The Thracian king, habituated to greed,
Was taken in and came to the hiding place,
Saying with smooth, practiced cunning,

                                "Quickly, Hecuba,   670
Give me the treasure for your son. All will be his,
What you give now and what you gave before,
I swear by the gods above."

                    She snarled at him
As he swore his lying oath, and then her rage
Boiled over. Calling the captive women in,
She seized the man and, digging her fingers
Into his lying eyes, she gouged them out.
Anger lent her strength, and plunging her hands
Deep inside, grimy with his guilty blood,
She sucked out not his eyes, for they were gone,   680
But the sockets themselves. The Thracian men,
Enraged by the slaughter of their king, attacked

The Trojan woman, hurling stones and weapons,
But she growled and snapped at the stones they threw,
And when she set her jaws to speak could only bark.
The place is still there and takes its name, Cynossema,
The Bitch's Tomb, from what happened there,
And for a long time she howled mournfully
Through the Sithonian plains, remembering
Her ancient wrongs. Her fate moved the Trojans   690
And her enemies the Greeks, and it moved the gods,
All the gods, for even Juno, Jove's sister and wife,
Said Hecuba had never deserved such an end.

★ ★ ★

Galatea and Polyphemus

*[The sea nymph Galatea tells the story of the Cyclops Polyphemus'
infatuation with her.]*

Faunus had a son by the nymph Symaethis.
Acis was his name, and he was a great delight   900
To his father and mother, but more so to me,
Since he and I loved only each other.
He was handsome, just sixteen, a faint down
On his tender cheeks. While I only went for him,
The Cyclops only went for me, relentlessly.
If you asked me I could not say whether
Love for Acis or hatred of the Cyclops
Was stronger in me. Both were just as strong.
O sweet Venus, how powerfully you rule us.
That savage, a horror to the woods themselves,   910
Whom no stranger has ever laid eyes on
Without getting hurt, who scorns great Olympus
And its gods, how strongly he feels just what love is,
How he burns, a prisoner of desire so passionate
He forgets his cave and his flocks. Now, Polyphemus,

You care about how you look, anxious to please.
Now you comb your bristling hair with a rake
And trim your rough beard with a scythe, gazing
At your face in a farm pond and taking care
To compose your expression. Your love of killing,   920
Your ferocity, your immense thirst for blood
Are gone, and ships now can sail by in safety.

During this time Telemus had traveled
To Sicilian Aetna, Telemus Eurymides,
Who knew what meaning every bird portended.
This augur addressed Polyphemus and said,
"That one eye in the middle of your forehead—
Ulysses will steal it." The Cyclops laughed, saying
"Stupid seer, someone has already stolen it."
Scoffing at the man who had tried to warn him,   930
He plodded heavily along the seashore
Or returned wearily to his shadowy cave.
There was a wedge-shaped hill with a high ridge
Jutting into the sea, washed by waves on both sides.
The beastly Cyclops climbed up to the top
And sat himself down. His sheep followed him
All on their own. Then, laying at his feet
The trunk of a pine that served as his staff,
Big as a ship's mast, he picked up his pipe
Made of a hundred bound reeds. All the mountains   940
Felt the sound of his pastoral pipings,
And the waves felt it too. I heard it myself
From a faraway cliff as I lay with my head
In Acis' lap, and I remember his song:

"Galatea, whiter than privet petals,
Slimmer than an alder, more in bloom
Than a meadow, friskier than a kid,
More radiant than crystal, smoother than shells
Polished by the tide, more welcome than shade
In the summer, than sunshine in winter,   950
Prettier than a plane tree, nimbler than a gazelle,

More sparkling than ice, sweeter than ripe grapes,
Softer than swan's down or curdled milk,
Lovelier than a watered garden, if you did not flee.

Galatea, wilder than an untamed heifer,
Harder than old oak, more slippery than water,
Tougher than willow or twisting vines,
More stubborn than cliffs, roiling more than a river,
Vainer than a peacock, fiercer than fire,
Meaner than a pregnant bear, pricklier   960
Than thistles, deafer than the sea, more vicious
Than a snake that's been stepped on and kicked;
And what I wish I could change most of all,
Swifter than a deer driven on by loud baying,
Swifter than the wind or a fleeting breeze.

But if you really knew me, O Galatea,
You'd be sorry you ran, renounce putting me off
And try your best to hold on to me.
I have most of a mountain, with deep caves
Where you don't feel the heat of the sun in summer   970
Nor winter's cold. I have apples weighing down
Their branches, golden grapes on long trailing vines,
Purple grapes too. I'm keeping both kinds for you.
You can pick ripe strawberries in the shady woods,
Cherries in the autumn, and plums, purple-black
And juicy, and the large yellow kind, yellow as wax.
If I can just be your man, you will have chestnuts too,
And arbute berries. Every tree will serve you.

And this whole flock is mine, many more too,
Browsing the valleys and wandering the woods,   980
And still others safe in their folds in the caves.
Don't ask me how many, I could not tell you
How many. Only poor people count up their flocks.
You don't have to believe me, you can see for yourself
How fine they are, how they can hardly walk
With their swollen udders. And I have lambs

In their warm pens, and kids too, all the same ages
Kept in separate pens. There's always plenty of milk,
White as snow, some of it kept for drinking,
And some of it rennet hardens into curds.   990

And you will not have any ordinary pets
Like does, rabbits, goats, a pair of doves
Or a nest from a treetop. I just found
A pair of bear cubs up on the mountain
For you to play with, so much alike
You can hardly tell them apart. When I found them
I said, 'These I'll save for my mistress.'

Just raise your glistening head, Galatea,
From the deep blue sea and come to me!
Don't hate my gifts. I know what I look like. I saw   1000
My reflection in a clear pool, and I liked what I saw.
Just look how big I am! Jupiter's no bigger,
Since you're always talking about some Jupiter
Who rules up in the sky. I have lots of hair
On my fierce looking face, down to my shoulders
Like a shady grove. And don't think I am ugly
Because my whole body bristles with hair.
A tree without any leaves is ugly, a horse
Is ugly without a golden mane on its neck;
Feathers cover birds; wool looks nice on sheep,   1010
And a beard and long hair look nice on a man.
I have only one eye in my forehead's middle,
But it's a big eye, as big as a shield! So?
Doesn't the Sun see all there is from the sky?
And doesn't the Sun have only one eye?
More, my father Neptune rules your waters,
And I'm giving him to you as a father-in-law.
Just pity me and hear my humble prayer,
For I bend my knee to you alone. I,
Who scorn Jupiter, his sky, and his thunderbolt,   1020
Fear you alone, O Nereid! Your anger
Is fiercer than lightning. And I could endure

Your contempt more easily if you also scorned
Your other suitors as well. Tell me why,
When you turn your back on Cyclops, you love
Acis, and why do you prefer his embrace to mine?
He can please himself, and what I don't like,
Galatea, please you as well. Just let me at him!
He'll find out I'm as strong as I am big.
I'll rip his guts out alive, and tear him apart   1030
Limb from limb, and scatter the pieces
All over the fields and over your waves.
Let him mate with you then! Oh, I'm burning up,
Just boiling mad. I feel like I have Aetna
Pent up inside me, with all of its power,
And you, Galatea, you don't even care!"

He went on with this drivel and then rose
Like a bull that is furious (I saw all of this)
Because his cow has been taken away.
Restless, he wandered the woods and pastures,   1040
Until, to my utter surprise, the big brute
Caught sight of me with Acis. "I see you," he said,
"And I'll fix it so this is the last time you make love."
His voice was as loud and as awful
As only a Cyclops' voice can be. Aetna
Trembled at the sound. As for me, I panicked
And dove into the sea. My hero, Symaethis' son,
Had already turned his back and started to run,
Crying,
        "Galatea, help me! Mother and Father,
I am about to die, take me into your world!"   1050

Cyclops stayed on him and hurled a rock
He had wrenched from the mountain. Although
The rock's very tip was all that hit Acis,
It was enough to bury the boy completely.
I did the only thing the fates allowed me to do,
Caused Acis to assume his ancestral powers.
Crimson blood seeped out from the massive rock,

And in a little while the color began to fade,
Looking at first like a rain-swollen river
And then slowly running clear. Then the rock   1060
Split open. A tall green reed grew from the crack,
And leaping waters resounded in a cavity
That formed in the stone, and then, more wonderful still,
A youth stood waist-deep in the water, his new horns
Wreathed with rushes. Though he was bigger,
And his face was deep blue, it could have been Acis,
And in fact it was Acis, changed to a river god,
And his waters retained his name of old.

★ ★ ★

Book 14

★ ★ ★

The Death of Aeneas

[Aeneas has brought his band of Trojan refugees to Italy and, victorious in war there, has founded the city of Lavinium, the cradle of Rome and its empire.]

Aeneas' virtue had now moved all the gods,
Even Juno herself, to set aside their old grudges,
And since his son Iulus was growing up
And his fortunes well established, the time was ripe
For Venus' heroic son to enter heaven.
She had lobbied all the gods, and throwing her arms
Around her father's neck she said,
                                        "O Father,
You have never been harsh to me, and I pray
That you will be most kind now. Grant my Aeneas—
Your grandson, O Supreme Lord, and of our blood—   680
Some divinity, however slight, but some at least.
Once is enough for him to have looked upon
That unlovely realm, to have crossed the Styx once."

And Father Jupiter replied,
                                "You are worthy
Of such divine favor, both you and he for whom
You ask. You may have what you desire, daughter."

Venus was exultant. She thanked her father
And then, borne through the air by her doves,
Came to the coast where the Numicius
Winds through reeds and pours its fresh water   690

Into the Laurentian sea. She asked the river god
To wash away all of Aeneas' mortality
And carry it in his silent stream into the deep.
The horned god obeyed, and he cleansed Aeneas
Of all that was mortal. His best part remained.
His mother anointed him with divine perfume,
Touched his lips with ambrosia and nectar
And so made him a god. The Romans called him
Indiges, and honored him with a temple and altars.

Under Ascanius the state was called both   700
Alban and Latin. Silvius succeeded him,
And his son Latinus took the name inherited
With the ancient scepter. Illustrious Alba
Succeeded Latinus; Epytus was next,
And then, in order, Capys and Capetus.
Tiberinus received the kingdom from them,
And when he drowned in the old Tuscan stream
He gave the river his name. His sons were called
Remulus and Acrota. Remulus, the elder,
Was struck by lightning while he was trying   710
To imitate thunder. Acrota, less arrogant,
Passed on the scepter to brave Aventinus,
Who lies buried on the hill where he had his palace
And that still bears his name. And now it was Proca
Who reigned supreme over the Palatine race.

Pomona and Vertumnus

Pomona lived under this king. No other
Latian wood nymph knew more about gardens
Or was more zealous in tending an orchard,
Whence her name. She was not interested
In forests or rivers; she loved the fields   720
And trees laden with delicious ripe fruit.
Her hand held no javelin, but a pruning hook
With which she restrained luxuriant growth,
Cut back spreading branches, or made in the bark

An incision for grafting a twig in a branch
To give it fresh sap. She kept all her trees
Well watered, irrigating their thirsty roots.
This was her love, this was all her desire,
And she had no interest in Venus at all.
But she did fear rape, and shut herself up   730
Inside her orchard, keeping men at a distance.
The dancing satyrs did everything they could
To win her hand, as did the pine-wreathed Pans.
And Silvanus, always younger than his age,
And Priapus, who scares off thieves with his sickle
Or his virile shaft. Vertumnus outdid them all
In the art of love, but came off no better.
How many times did he come dressed as a reaper
And bring her a basket full of barley ears?
And he would really look like a reaper, too.   740
Or he would come with fresh hay wreathing his head,
And you would think he had just been turning
The new-mown grass. Or he would have an ox-goad
In his calloused hand, and you would swear
He had just unyoked his weary team. He would be
A vine-dresser carrying a pruning hook,
Or show up with a ladder, so you would think
He was going to pick apples. He could be
A soldier with a sword, a fisherman with a pole.
With all these disguises he got to see her a lot,   750
And he loved the beauty he saw. Once he put on
A wig of grey hair, bound with a colorful scarf,
And leaning on a staff came as an old woman
Into the immaculate orchard, and said,
As he admired the fruit, "But you are much better."
And he kissed her two or three times, kisses such as
No real old woman would ever have given.
Then, all hunched over, he sat on the grass
And gazed at the branches heavy with autumn's fruit.
There was a shapely elm opposite, draped   760
With gleaming clusters of grapes. He looked at the tree

And its companion vine with an approving eye
And then said,
        "You know, if that tree stood there
Unwed to the vine, it would only have leaves,
Not much use; and the vine, that now clings to the elm
And rests nicely there, if it were not mated
To the tree, would just lie flat on the ground.
But you don't take the vine's example, do you?
You shun wedlock and don't care about a mate.
I wish you did. Then you would have more suitors   770
Than Helen had, or than Hippodameia,
For whom the Lapiths fought, or Penelope,
The wife of the late-returning Ulysses.
Even now, although you hold them in contempt,
A thousand men want you, and all the gods,
Spirits, and demigods that haunt the Alban hills.
But if you are wise and want to make a good match
And would listen to this old woman—who loves you
More than all the rest, more than you can believe—
You would reject all the common offers of marriage   780
And choose Vertumnus for your bedmate.
I can vouch for him, for he is not better known
Even to himself than he is to me.
He doesn't wander the wide world, but stays here
In this neighborhood. Nor does he fall in love
With whatever he sees, unlike most of your suitors.
You will be his first love and his last; you will be
The love of his life. Then too, he is young,
Charming, and can assume any form he likes
And whatever form you want. Moreover,   790
You like the same things, and he is the first to have
Your favorite fruit, and he lights up at your gifts.
But it is neither the fruit from your trees,
Nor the juicy greens that you grow in your garden
Nor anything else except you he desires.
Pity the lover, and believe that he himself
Is courting you through the words I am speaking.
And do respect the avenging gods, and Venus,

Who detests the hard-hearted, and Nemesis,
Who never forgets. And so you will respect them more,   800
Let me tell you (I've learned a thing or two in my time)
A story that is well known all over Cyprus.
It may teach you to bend and to be softer of heart.

Iphis and Anaxarete

Iphis, a boy of humble birth, chanced to see
Anaxarete once, a girl from the old family
Of Teucer in Salamis. As soon as he saw her
Love's fire shot through his bones. He fought it,
But when reason failed to overcome his passion,
He came to her door as a suppliant. First he confided
In the nurse, confessing his love and begging her   810
In the name of all her hopes for her foster child
Not to be hard on him. Then he tried to coax
The servants to put in a good word for him,
Writing sweet talk on tablets for them to pass on.
Sometimes he would hang garlands of flowers
On her door, first wetting them with his tears,
And then lay his soft body on her hard threshold
And utter complaints to her door's grim bars.
Harsher than the sea surge when the Goat Stars set,
Harder than steel tempered in a Noric forge   820
Or than living rock embedded in the earth,
She spurns him and mocks him, adding insults
And abusive language to heartless rejection,
And leaves her lover utterly deprived of hope.
Unable to endure the torment any longer,
Iphis called out his last words before her door:

'You win, Anaxarete; you won't have to put up
With me any longer. Celebrate your victory,
Sing songs of triumph, wear a laurel wreath
On your head, for you have really won,   830
And I will gladly die. Let your iron heart rejoice.
You will be compelled to praise something about me,
Some way I was pleasing, some merit I had.

But remember, my love did not end before my life
And I lost two lights at once. No rumor
Will bring you news of my death. I will be there
In person, so you can feast your cruel eyes
On my lifeless corpse.
                    And yet, O gods,
If you see what mortals do, let me be
Remembered (I cannot bear to ask for more),   840
Let my story be told in future ages
And add to my fame the years you took from my life.'

Iphis said these things, and lifted his tear-filled eyes
To the doorposts on which he had often hung
Garlands of flowers, and raising his pale arms
He tied a rope to the crossbeam, saying,
'This wreath will please you, cruel as you are.'
Then he put his head in the noose, which soon
Crushed his windpipe. And even as he hung there,
The pitiful weight of his body turned slowly   850
To face her, and his feet knocked against the door
As if he were requesting to enter; and when
The door was opened, it revealed what he had done.

The servants shrieked, and lifted him from the noose,
But all in vain. Then they carried his body
To his mother's house, since his father was dead,
And she took him to her breast, enfolding her arms
Around her son's cold limbs. And when she had said
All the things that distraught parents would say,
And done all the things distraught mothers do,   860
His funeral procession wound through the city's streets
As she took his pale corpse on a bier to the pyre.

The sad procession happened to pass the house
Of Anaxarete, and the sound of mourning
Rose to her ears. It must have been some vengeful god
Who roused her stony heart, but she was roused
And said, 'Let's take a look at this wretched funeral,'
As she went to a rooftop room with a view.

She had barely caught sight of Iphis on the pallet,
When her eyes became fixed, and the blood drained   870
From her pallid body. She tried to step back
But was rooted to the spot and could not even
Turn her face away. The stoniness that had long
Been deep in her heart now slowly crept over
Her body as well. If you think this is only
An old wives' tale, there is still in Salamis
A statue of the woman, as well as a temple
Of Gazing Venus. Keep all this in mind,
O nymph of mine. Put aside your stubborn pride
And embrace your lover. That way you'll be sure   880
That the frost won't nip your apples in the bud,
Nor the storm winds scatter your peach blossoms."

Pomona and Vertumnus (continued)

Vertumnus said all this dressed as an old woman,
But to no effect. He then threw off his disguise
And became himself again, appearing to Pomona
As a shining youth. It was as if the sun
Had emerged resplendent from a bank of clouds
And shone unblemished in the sky. He was ready
To force her, but no force was needed. The nymph
Responded to the god with an equal passion.   890

The Sabines

Amulius now rules Italy, with unjust use
Of military might, and then old Numitor
Aided by his grandson Romulus, retakes
His lost kingdom, and Rome is founded
On the feast day of Pales, god of shepherds.

The Sabines under Tatius wage war on Rome,
And Tarpeia, who opened the city to them,
Loses her life under a crush of weapons.

Then while the Romans lie buried in sleep,
The men of Cures, like silent wolves, advance   900
With hushed voices and try the city's gates

That Romulus has barred. Juno herself
Unfastens one of these, and the gate swings open
Without a sound. Venus alone perceived
That the bar had fallen and would have replaced it,
But a god may not undo another god's deed.
Right next to Janus' shrine, though, the Ausonian nymphs
Had a spot where a cold spring bubbled up.
Venus enlisted their aid, and the nymphs complied,
Opening their spring's channels. Up until then   910
The pass of Janus had never been closed
Or the road blocked by water, but now the nymphs
Stoked the source of their spring with yellow sulphur
And heated the channels with burning pitch,
So that the pool was steaming down to its depths,
And the water that had been as cold as the Alps
Was as hot as fire. The gateposts smoldered
Under a fiery spray, and the gate itself,
By which the tough Sabines had thought to enter
Was impassable with water, giving the Romans   920
Time to arm themselves. Then Romulus attacked,
And soon the Roman fields were strewn with Sabine dead
As well as the bodies of their native sons,
And those impious swords mingled the blood of Romans
With the Sabine blood of their wives' fathers.
But the war ended with a truce, and it was agreed
That Tatius would share the Roman throne.

Romulus

When Tatius died, you, Romulus, governed
Both peoples with equal justice. Then Mars set aside
His gleaming helmet and in these words addressed   930
The Father of Gods and Men:
                              "The time has come,
Father, since Rome now stands on firm foundations
And does not depend on just one man, for you to grant
The promised reward to me and your grandson,
To free his spirit and set him in the heavens.
You once spoke to me at a council of the gods
Gracious words I remember and keep in my mind,

'There will be one you will raise to heaven's azure.'
Now let the sum of your words at last be fulfilled."

Almighty Jupiter nodded, and veiling the sky   940
With dark clouds, he terrified the men on earth
With thunder and lightning. Mars recognized this
As a sign of the promised ascension to heaven,
And leaning on his spear, he vaulted fearlessly
Into his bloodstained chariot and cracked the whip
Above the straining horses. Gliding steeply down,
He landed on the Palatine's wooded summit.
There, as Ilia's son was dealing royal justice,
Mars caught him up. His mortal body dissipated
Into thin air, the way a lead bullet hurled   950
By a sling can melt into the endless sky.
Beautiful now, he is Quirinus, robed and worthier
To take his place at the gods' high couches.

Hersilia

His wife Hersilia mourned him as lost
Until royal Juno ordered Iris to go down
On her curving path and bear this message
To the grieving widow:
                            "O glory of both
The Latin and the Sabine people, worthy
To have been the wife of so great a hero
And now of Quirinus, dry your tears,   960
And if you desire to see your husband,
Follow me to the grove on the Quirinal Hill
That shades the temple of the king of Rome."

Iris obeyed and, gliding down to earth
Along the arch of her iridescent bow,
She delivered the message to Hersilia,
Who barely lifted her eyes when she answered,

"Goddess—I cannot easily tell who you are,
But you are clearly a goddess—lead on,
Oh, lead on, and show me my husband's face.   970

If the Fates allow me to see him just once,
I will declare that he has been taken to heaven."

And without delay she went with Thaumas' daughter
To the hill of Romulus, where a star fell,
Gliding down to earth through the pure sky,
And Hersilia, her hair bursting into flames
From its light, disappeared up into the air
Along with the star. The founder of Rome
Enfolded her in his familiar embrace
And changed her in body and name, calling her   980
Hora, a goddess united with her Quirinus.

Book 15

★ ★ ★

Aesculapius

Reveal to me now, Muses, divine ones
Present to poets (for you know, and time
Does not cheat you) how did Aesculapius
Come to the island lapped by the deep Tiber
And be set among the deities of Rome?

Long ago a plague had infected Latium's air,
And the people wasted away with a ghastly disease.
Weary with caring for the dead, and seeing   690
That their human efforts and the physicians' arts
Accomplished nothing, they sought heaven's aid.
Coming to Delphi, the oracle of Phoebus
In the center of the earth, they prayed for a response
That would save them from their suffering and end
The great city's woes. The shrine and the laurel,
And the god's quiver itself, began to tremble,
And the tripod deep in the inner sanctum
Uttered words that made their hearts shake with fear:

"What you seek here, Romans, you should have sought   700
From a closer place. Seek now from some place closer.
Nor do you need Apollo to lessen your troubles,
But Apollo's son, under good auspices sought."

When the Senate in its wisdom heard the oracle,
They found out which city the god's son lived in
And sent an embassy to sail to Epidaurus.
When they had beached their ship on that shore
The ambassadors petitioned the council of elders

To give them the deity whose presence in Rome
Would stop the destruction of the Ausonian race,   710
As the oracle had distinctly pronounced.
The elders held conflicting opinions.
Some thought that the aid should not be denied,
But many advised that they should keep their god
And not surrender the source of their wealth
Or their deity. While they deliberated,
Dusk dispelled the lingering light, and when
Darkness spread shadows all over the world,
The god of healing appeared in your dreams,
O Roman ambassador, standing by your bed   720
Just as he appears in his own temple,
Holding in his left hand a rustic staff
And stroking his flowing beard with his right.
And with a calm presence he uttered these words:

"Have no fear! I will leave my shrine and come.
Just look at this serpent entwining my staff
And fix it in your mind. I will change myself
Into this form, but larger, and will seem as great
As celestial bodies should when they change."

The god left with his voice, and with voice and god   730
The dream left too, and as sleep slipped away
The kindly day dawned and put the stars to flight.
The council, still undecided, assembled
At the magnificent temple of the god in question
And begged him to reveal by signs from heaven
Where he himself wanted to have his home.
They had just finished when the golden god,
In the form of a serpent with a soaring crest,
Signaled his presence by hissing, and at his coming
He shook the statue, the altars, the doors,   740
The marble floor, and the golden rooftop.
Then, arching breast-high in the temple's court,
He surveyed the scene with eyes that flashed fire.
Everyone trembled with fear, but the priest,

His hair bound with a white woolen fillet,
Recognized the divinity and cried,

"The god! Behold the god! Be pure of heart
And observe reverent silence, all who are present.
And, O most beautiful one, may this vision
Be beneficial, and bless all your faithful."   750

The whole congregation worshipped the god,
Repeating the priest's prayer, and the Romans too
Were reverential in the words of their lips
And the meditations of their hearts.
His crest rippled as the god nodded to them
And hissed three times with his flickering tongue
To affirm his pledge. Then he glided down
The polished steps and turned to gaze one last time
Upon the ancient altars he was now leaving,
And he saluted the temple that had long been his home.   760
From there the huge serpent wound his way along
The flower-strewn ground, coiling through the city
To the curved walls of the harbor. Here he paused,
And, with a look of perfect serenity,
Seemed to dismiss his devout throng of followers
Before he boarded the Ausonian ship. It felt
The deity's burden, and the keel sank down
Under the god's weight. The Romans were overjoyed,
And, after sacrificing a bull on the shore,
Wreathed their ship with flowers and then cast off.   770
A light breeze pushed her on. The god rose high,
And resting his neck upon the curved stern,
Gazed down upon the indigo water. Favorable winds
Took him across the Ionian Sea, and the sixth dawn
Saw him reach Italy. He sailed past Juno's temple
On the shore of Lacinium, past Sylaceum,
Left Iapygia behind, and avoiding on portside
The Amphrisian rocks, and on the starboard
The Cocinthian cliffs, skirted Romethium,
Caulon and Narycia, got through the straits   780

Of Sicily and Pelorus' narrows, sailed past
The home of Hippotades, past Temesa
And its copper mines, then made for Leucosia
And the rose gardens of Paestum. From there
He rounded Capreae, Minerva's promontory,
And vineyards on the hills of Surrentum;
Then on to Herculaneum, on to Stabiae
And to Parthenope, the city of Naples,
Founded for pleasure, and from there to the temple
Of the Cumaean Sibyl. Next Baiae's hot springs   790
And the mastic groves of Liternum, and the mouth
Of the Volturnus River, churning with sand;
Then Sinuessa, with its flocks of white doves,
Grim Minturnae, and Caieta, where Aeneas
Buried his nurse; the home of Antiphates,
Marshy Trachas, the land of Circe also,
And the heavily sanded beach of Antium.
The sea was rough when the sailors put in here,
So the god unfolded his coils, and, gliding on
With great sinuous curves, entered the temple   800
Of his father Apollo there on the shore.
When the sea was calm again, Aesculapius,
Having enjoyed familial hospitality,
Left his father's altars and furrowed the beach
With his rasping scales, and climbing the rudder
Rested his head on the ship's high stern
Until he came to Castrum, the Tiber's mouth
And the sacred seats of Lavinium.
The entire population came to meet him,
A throng of mothers and fathers, and the virgins   810
Who tend your fires, O Trojan Vesta,
And they greeted the god with joy. As the ship
Floated upstream, incense burned and crackled
On a row of altars built on both banks.
The smoke scented the air; and the blood
Of sacrificial victims warmed the knives at their throats.
And now the ship entered the city of Rome,

Capital of the world. The serpent reared up,
And, resting his head on the top of the mast,
Looked around for a good site for his temple.   820
The river here splits into two branches,
Forming the area known as the Island,
Stretching two equal arms around the land between.
This is where the serpentine son of Phoebus
Disembarked from the Latian ship, and resuming
His celestial form he came to the Romans
As the god who brings health, and ended their sorrows.

The Deification of Caesar

This god came to our shrines from a foreign land,
But Caesar is a god in his own city.
Illustrious in war and peace, his conversion   830
Into a new constellation and into a comet
Was caused not as much by his triumph in war,
Or his civic achievements, or his rise to glory
As by his progeny. For in all Caesar has done,
Nothing is greater than this, that he became
The father of our emperor. For is it greater
To have subdued the island of Britain,
To have led his victorious fleet up the Nile,
To have added the rebellious Numidians,
Libyan Juba, and Pontus shouting "Mithridates!"   840
To the people of Romulus, to have celebrated
Numerous triumphs and deserved many more—
Than to have brought forth such a great man,
The ruler of the world, and your richest blessing,
O gods above, upon the human race?
And so, that his son not have a mortal father,
It was necessary for Caesar to become a god.

When the golden mother of Aeneas saw this,
And saw also that an armed conspiracy
Was plotting the death of the high priest, Caesar,   850
She paled, and cried to each god she met,

"Look at this mountain of treachery upon me,
And the insidious designs upon the one person
Who is all I have left of Dardanian Iulus.
Shall I alone be forever persecuted?
Wounded by Diomedes' Calydonian spear,
The walls of my poorly defended Troy
Falling around me, my son wandering in exile,
Battered on the sea, descending to the realm
Of the silent shades, waging war with Turnus,   860
Or to tell the truth, waging war with Juno!
My present fears do not permit reminiscing.
Look at the impious swords being sharpened.
Stop them! Ward off this crime! Do not extinguish
The fires of Vesta with the blood of her priest!"

Venus flung her anxieties through all of heaven,
But to no effect. Although the gods were moved,
They were powerless against the iron decrees
Of the ancient sisters. Still, they could give
Unmistakable portents of the grief to come.   870
They say that arms clashing in black storm clouds
And the frightening sound of horns in the sky
Forewarned men of the crime. The sun's face dimmed
And gave lurid light upon the troubled lands.
Firebrands were seen burning among stars in the sky,
And drops of blood rained down from the clouds.
The Morning Star darkened and turned dull red,
And the Moon's chariot was stained with blood.
The Stygian owl hooted its mournful omens
In a thousand places, and ivory statues   880
In thousands of places dripped with tears.
Dirges and threats are said to have been heard
In sacred groves. No sacrifices were auspicious.
The liver warned that terrible upheavals
Were about to begin, and its cleft lobe
Was found in the entrails. Dogs howled at night
In the market place, around men's houses
And the temples of the gods; silent shades

Walked abroad, and earthquakes shook the city.
But the gods' warnings were not able to overcome   890
The treachery of men and destiny unfolding.
Naked swords were brought into the sacred Curia,
For no other place in the entire city
Pleased the conspirators for this heinous slaughter.
Then indeed did the Cytherean beat her breast
And tried to hide the descendant of Aeneas
In the same kind of cloud that of old saved Paris
From murderous Menelaus, and that allowed
Aeneas himself to escape Diomedes' sword.
But then Jupiter spoke:
                              "Will you on your own,   900
My child, try to move insuperable Fate?
You may go yourself into the three sisters' house.
There will you see a massive account of the world
Inscribed on tablets of solid iron and brass
That fear in their eternal and total immunity
Neither conflict with heaven, nor lightning's wrath,
Nor any ruin or collapse whatsoever.
And there on everlasting adamant
You will find engraved your descendants' fates.
I have read these myself and made mental note   910
And will now relate them so that you will no longer
Be ignorant of the future.
                              The man, Cytherea,
For whom you struggle has completed the years
He owes to the earth. You will bring about
His entrance to heaven and his worship in temples,
You and his son. He will succeed to the name
And will alone bear the burden placed upon him,
And with ourselves as his allies in war,
Will be his slain father's heroic avenger.
Under his command besieged Mutina   920
Will sue for peace; Pharsalia will feel his power;
The fields of Philippi in Macedonia
Will be drenched in blood again; Sextus Pompeius
Will be defeated off Sicily's coast;

And Cleopatra, the Egyptian mistress
Of a Roman general, her faith misplaced
In their alliance, will fall before the son of Caesar
Despite all her vain threats to transfer our Capitol
To her Canopus.
                        I will not mention
The barbarous nations on both shores of the ocean,   930
But every habitable land on earth
Will be under his sway, and the ocean too!
And when peace has been bestowed on all these lands
He will turn his mind to the rights of citizens
And establish laws most just, and by his example
Guide the way men behave. Looking to the future
And generations to come, he will pass on his name
And his burdens as well to the son born to him
And to his chaste wife. And not until he is old
And his years equal his meritorious actions   940
Will he go to heaven and his familial stars.
In the meantime, catch up this Caesar's soul
As it leaves his slain body and make it a star,
So that the divine Julius may ever look forth
Upon our Capitol and Forum from his high temple."

He had scarcely finished when kindly Venus,
Standing in the senate house, invisible to all,
Caught her Caesar's soul as it left his body,
And not allowing it to diffuse in the air,
She bore it upward to the stars of heaven.   950
And while she carried it she felt it glow
And grow warm, and sent it forth from her bosom.
It soared higher than the moon, trailing fire
Behind it, and shone as a star. And now he sees
All his son's good deeds and confesses that
They are greater than his own, and he rejoices
To be surpassed by him. And though the son forbids
His own deeds to be ranked above his father's,
Fame, free and obedient to no one's command,
Puts him forward, only in this opposing his will.   960

So does Atreus yield to his son Agamemnon,
So Aegeus to Theseus, and Peleus to Achilles,
And to cite last an instance that suits them both,
So too is Saturn a lesser god than Jove.
And as Jupiter is in control of high heaven
And the realms of the triple world, the earth
Is under Augustus, as both ruler and sire.

O gods, I pray: comrades of Aeneas,
Before whom fire and sword gave way;
Gods of Italy, and you, Romulus,   970
The father of our city; and Mars,
Invincible sire of Romulus; Vesta,
Revered among Caesar's household gods;
Apollo, worshipped along with Caesar's Vesta;
Jupiter exalted on Tarpeia's rock;
And all other gods to whom it is right and just
For a poet to pray:
                      May the day come late
And after our own time, when Augustus,
Abandoning the world he rules, enters
High heaven and hears our prayers from above.   980

Envoi

And now I have completed my work,
Which cannot be undone by the wrath of Jove,
By fire or sword, or corrosive time. That final day,
Which has power only over my body,
May come when it will and end my uncertain
Span of years. The better part of me
Will be borne forever beyond the high stars,
And my name will never die. Wherever Rome
Extends its power over the conquered world
I will be on men's lips, and if a sacred poet   990
Has any power to prophesy the truth,
Throughout the ages I will live on in fame.

Glossary of Main Characters

Actae'on: son of Autonoë and grandson of Cadmus, killed by his hounds after seeing Diana while she was bathing

Ado'nis: son of his grandfather Cinyras and his sister Myrrha; beloved by Venus; memorialized as a flower

Ae'acus: son of Jupiter and Aegina; pious king of the island Aegina

Aene'as: Trojan hero, son of Venus and Anchises; father of Ascanius; legendary founder of Rome. Led Trojan survivors to Italy, where he was deified as Indiges

Aescula'pius: son of Apollo and Coronis; a mortal deified as the god of healing; associated with the serpent

Aga've: daughter of Cadmus. Killed her son Pentheus during a Bacchic frenzy

Age'nor: king of Sidon; son of Neptune; father of Europa and Cadmus

Alphe'us: primary river of Elis. River god who loved Arethusa

Althe'a: wife of Oeneus. It was foretold at her son Meleager's birth that his fate was tied to a certain log in the fireplace. In horror and rage at Meleager's slaying of her brothers, Althea set fire to the log and thus killed her son

A'mor: a name for Cupid

Amphitri'te: sea goddess, wife of Neptune; mother of Triton

Anaxar'ete: girl of noble birth. Rejected the love of Iphis and was turned to stone

Andro'meda: daughter of Cassiopeia and Cepheus; rescued from chains by Perseus and placed in the stars by Minerva

Apol'lo (Phoe'bus): son of Jupiter and Latona; twin brother of Diana, associated with the oracle at Delphi; god of the sun, prophecy, youth, and medicine

Arach'ne: famous weaver from Lydia. Lost a weaving contest with Minerva, who transformed her into a spider

Ar'cas: son of Jupiter and Callisto

Arethu′sa: nymph of Elis, pursued by Alpheus; transformed into a spring by Diana

Ar′gus: monstrous son of Arestor. Guarded Io until being killed by Mercury

Ariad′ne: daughter of Minos; deserted by Theseus after helping him escape the Labyrinth. The crown constellation Corona Borealis was placed in the sky by her rescuer Bacchus in her honor

Astrae′a: a goddess of justice

Atalan′ta: daughter of Schoenus; huntress of Arcadia. Her marriage to Hippomenes ended tragically as foretold by an oracle

At′las: son of the Titan Iapetus; father of the Pleiades and Calypso. Holds up the sky

Augus′tus: Gaius Julius Caesar Octavianus Augustus, known as Augustus beginning in 27 BCE. Adopted son of Julius Caesar; first emperor of Rome, from 31 BCE to 14 CE

Auro′ra: goddess of morning and the dawn, mother of Memnon

Aus′ter: the South Wind

Auton′oë: daughter of Cadmus; mother of Actaeon

Bac′chus (Li′ber, Diony′sus): son of Jupiter by Semele, sewn into Jupiter's thigh after Semele's death; a god associated with wine, pleasure, and the frenetic revelry of his followers

Bau′cis: wife of Philemon. She and her husband hosted Jupiter and Mercury when they visited in the guise of mortals

Be′lus: an Egyptian king whose granddaughters murdered their husbands and were punished by continuously filling sieves with water in Hades

Bo′reas: the North Wind

Cad′mus: exiled son of Agenor, brother of Europa, husband of Harmonia; founder of Thebes

Cae′sar (Gaius Julius Caesar): military and political leader of the Roman republic. Regarded as a descendant of Venus; adoptive father of Augustus. Deified after his death in 44 BCE

Callis′to: Arcadian nymph raped by Jupiter and despised by Juno; mother of Arcas

Ceph′alus: a prince of Athens and grandson of Aeolus; husband of Procris

Ce′pheus: Ethiopian king, father of Andromeda; placed in the stars by Neptune

Cer´berus: three-headed guard dog of Hades; briefly forced from Hades by Hercules

Ce´res (Deme´ter, De´o): goddess of fertility, grain, and food; mother of Proserpina by Jupiter

Chi´ron: immortal Centaur, son of Saturn and Philyra; father of Ocyrhoë by Chariclo. Caretaker of Aesculapius

Cin´yras: (1) a king of Assyria. His daughters were turned into the steps of Juno's temple as punishment for their pride; (2) father of Myrrha and of Adonis by Myrrha

Cleopa´tra: queen of Egypt and mistress of Mark Antony; defeated by Octavian (later known as Augustus)

Clyme´ne: daughter of Oceanus and Tethys; wife of the Ethiopian king Merops; mother of the Heliades, and of Phaëthon by Apollo

Cu´pid (A´mor, E´ros): god of love, son of Venus and Mars

Cybe´le: Phrygian mother goddess accompanied by lions. Desired Attis

Cy´gnus: son of Sthenelus; relative and friend of Phaëthon; transformed into a swan and placed in the sky as the constellation Cygnus

Daed´alus: Athenian artisan, father of Icarus; uncle of Perdix. Built a wooden cow for Pasiphaë and the Labyrinth for Minos

Da´naë: mother of Perseus by Jupiter after the god came to her as golden raindrops

Daph´ne: nymph daughter of Peneus, pursued by Apollo; transformed into a laurel tree

Deianei´ra: daughter of Oeneus; one of Meleager's two sisters not transformed into a guinea hen by his death; courted by Acheloüs and married to Hercules

Deuca´lion: pious son of Prometheus. Survived, with his wife Pyrrha, a flood sent by Jupiter

Dia´na (Ar´temis, Cyn´thia): daughter of Jupiter and Latona; sister of Apollo; born on the hill of Cynthus; goddess of fertility, wild animals, archery, and the moon

Diome´des: a Thracian king who killed men in order to feed his prized horses; defeated by Hercules

Dis: a name for Pluto

Ech´o: nymph whose control of her speech was taken away by Juno; smitten by helpless love for Narcissus

Ep´aphus: son of the deified Io by Jupiter; friend of Phaëthon

Erysi´chthon: impious Thessalian, punished with everlasting hunger for chopping down a tree of Ceres. Neptune granted his daughter the ability to change her form

Euro´pa: daughter of Agenor, Phoenician king; abducted by Jupiter in the form of a bull

Eu´rus: the East Wind

Eury´dice: wife of the musician Orpheus, who attempted to bargain her release from Hades after her death

Eurys´theus: Mycenaean king given mastery over Hercules as a result of Juno's deceit. Hercules was required to serve him by performing twelve labors

Fu´ries (Eri´nyes, Eume´nides): female spirits of retribution and vengeance; occasionally referred to as the three serpent-haired sisters Allecto, Tisiphone, and Megaera

Galate´a: nymph daughter of Nereus and Doris; beloved of Acis but desired by the Cyclops Polyphemus

Gan´ymede: Trojan boy loved by Jupiter, taken by the eagle of Jupiter to be the god's cupbearer

Ge´ryon: three-bodied, cattle-herding son of Medusa; killed by Hercules

Ha´des: the subterranean realm of the dead ruled by Pluto and Proserpina

Harmo´nia: daughter of Mars and Venus; wife of Cadmus

He´be: Juno's fatherless daughter; cupbearer of the gods, associated with youth; married to Hercules

Hec´ate: a goddess of the underworld and sorcery

Hec´uba: wife of Priam; mother of Hector, Paris, Polydorus, Helenus, Polyxena, and many others

Heli´ades: daughters of the sun god Helius by Clymene. Mourning their brother Phaëthon, the sisters were transformed into poplar trees with amber tears

Her´cules: son of Jupiter and Alcmena; completed twelve great labors under Eurystheus; killed by the Hydra's poisonous blood and placed in the stars as a constellation

Hermaphrodi´tus: son of Mercury and Venus; loved by the nymph Salmacis, became half-man, half-woman

Hersi´lia: wife of Romulus; deified as Hora

Hesper´ides: nymphs who guarded the garden of Juno's golden apples. Several apples were stolen by Hercules during his labors

Hippo´menes: husband of Atalanta; son of Megareus; transformed into a lion for an act of sacrilege against Cybele

Hyacin´thus: Spartan boy accidentally killed by Apollo; a flower grows from his blood as a symbol of Apollo's grief

Hy´men: the god of marriage

Hyperi´on: Titan father of the sun god Helius by Theia; an epithet of the sun god

Ic´arus: son of Daedalus. Wearing wings of wax and feathers, he fell to his death as he flew too close to the sun

In´achus: river and river god; father of Io

I´no: daughter of Cadmus; aunt of Bacchus and Pentheus; wife of Athamas

I´o: daughter of Inachus, assaulted by Jupiter and transformed into a heifer; called Isis in Egypt

Iola´us: nephew of Hercules, brought back to life as a youth by Hebe

I´phis: (1) daughter of Ligdus and Telethusa; raised as a boy so as not to be killed by her father; when betrothed to Ianthe, she was transformed into a boy by Isis; (2) boy of Cyprus; hanged himself due to unrequited love for Anaxarete

I´ris: messenger goddess of Juno, associated with the rainbow; daughter of Thaumas

I´sis: Egyptian goddess, sister and wife of Osiris; the deified Io

I´xion: Lapith king bound to a flaming, eternally revolving wheel as punishment for attempting to woo Juno; father of Pirithoüs and the Centaurs

Ja´nus: two-headed god of beginnings and thresholds; husband of Venilia

Jove: a name for Jupiter

Ju´no (Satur´nia, He´ra): wife and sister of Jupiter; patroness of women, marriage, and childbirth

Ju´piter (Jove, Zeus): son of Saturn; husband and brother of Juno; ruler of the Olympian gods; associated with the thunderbolt and its power

Lato´na (Le´to): Titaness daughter of Coeus; mother of Apollo and Diana by Jupiter

Le´da: wife of Tyndareus; mother of Castor, Pollux, Helen, and Clytemnestra by Jupiter, who came to her as a swan

Li´chas: servant of Hercules, killed by the hero after unwittingly presenting him with the Hydra's fatal blood

Liri´ope: water nymph and mother of Narcissus by Cephisus

Luci´na: goddess of childbirth

Lyca´on: early king of Arcadia; father of Callisto; transformed into a wolf by Jupiter

Mars (A´res): son of Jupiter and Juno; god of war; father of Romulus and Remus, legendary founders of Rome

Medu´sa: one of the Gorgons, daughter of Phorcys and loved by Neptune; became a serpent-headed creature so hideous that at a glance she turned mortals into stone

Melea´ger: son of Oeneus and Althea; leader in the Calydonian boar hunt

Mer´cury (Her´mes): son of Jupiter and the Pleiad Maia; father of Autolycus; messenger god, guide of souls to Hades; known for his cleverness and thievery

Mi´das: a Phrygian king; Bacchus granted his request for a golden touch

Miner´va (Pal´las, Trito´nia, Athe´na): virgin daughter of Jupiter; goddess of crafts, wisdom, and war; patron goddess of Athens

Mi´nos: son of Jupiter and Europa; husband of Pasiphaë; king of Crete

Mi´notaur: beast-child of Pasiphaë, born with the head of a bull; killed by Theseus in the Labyrinth

Muses: nine daughters of Jupiter and Mnemosyne (Memory); patron goddesses of the arts

Myr´rha: daughter of Cinyras; infatuated with her father; mother of his son Adonis

Narcis´sus: son of Cephisus and the raped nymph Liriope; beloved by Echo; infatuated with his own beauty

Ne´mesis: goddess of righteous anger and retribution

Nep´tune (Posei´don): god of the oceans and seas; brother of Jupiter, Juno, and Pluto

Ne´reus: a sea god who fathered fifty daughters, the Nereids

Nes´sus: centaur son of Ixion; killed by Hercules for attempting to assault Deianeira

Ni´sus: Megaran king whose single strand of purple hair was vital to his country's survival; betrayed by his daughter Scylla

Oce´anus: Titan god of the oceans; refused to fight the Olympians; fathered the Oceanids by his sister Tethys

Oed´ipus: Theban king, son of Laïus and Jocasta; unwittingly killed his father, winning his mother as wife when he solved the riddle of the Sphinx

Or´pheus: Thracian musician, son of the Muse Calliope; attempted to bring his wife Eurydice back from Hades; killed by Maenads

Osi´ris: Egyptian god of fertility; husband of Isis

Pai´on: epithet for Aesculapius, the god of healing and son of Apollo

Pan: half-goat god of shepherds and forests, originally Arcadian. Played a reed pipe

Pasi´phaë: daughter of the Sun; wife of Minos; mother of Ariadne, Phaedra, and the Minotaur

Per´seus: son of Jupiter and Danaë; slayer of Medusa. Rescued Andromeda

Pha´ëthon: son of Apollo and Clymene; killed attempting to drive his father's chariot across the sky

Phile´mon: elderly Phrygian; husband of Baucis. Humbly hosts Jupiter and Mercury

Philocte´tes: Greek warrior given his friend Hercules' bow

Philome´la: daughter of Pandion; sister of Procne; raped and mutilated by Tereus

Pho´cus: son of Aeacus and the Nereid Psamathe; killed by his half-brothers Telamon and Peleus, perhaps at the instigation of their mother

Phoe´be: Titaness mother of Latona and Asteria; grandmother of Apollo, Diana, and Hecate; also an epithet of Diana, referring to her association with the moon

Phoe´bus: an epithet of Apollo, referring to his association with the sun

Plei´ades: the seven daughters of Atlas, represented by the cluster of seven stars found in the constellation of Taurus

Plu´to (Dis, Or´cus): son of Saturn, brother of Jupiter and Neptune; god of the underworld

Pol´lux: son of Leda and Zeus; brother of Castor, Helen, and Clytemnestra. The two brothers are associated with the constellation Gemini

Polydo´rus: son of Priam and Hecuba; killed by the treacherous Thracian king Polymestor

Polyphe´mus: a Cyclops infatuated with Galatea

Poly´xena: daughter of Priam and Hecuba; sacrificed by the Greeks upon Achilles' tomb

Pomo´na: wood nymph of Latium; caretaker of fruit trees

Pompei´us, Sextus: son of Pompey the Great; defeated in naval battle by Augustus (then Octavian)

Proc´ne: daughter of Pandion; wife of Tereus and sister of Philomela; mother of Itys, whom she killed and fed to his father

Pro´cris: daughter of Erechtheus; wife of Cephalus; killed by her husband during a hunt

Prome´theus: Titan son of Iapetus and Themis, brother of Atlas. Created humans from clay; stole Olympian fire and gave it to humans

Pro´teus: prophetic sea god with the ability to change his form

Pygma´lion: Cyprian sculptor of an ivory woman, which was brought to life by Venus; father of Paphos

Pyr´rha: queen of Thessaly; wife of Deucalion and daughter of Epimetheus

Py´thon: serpent that held Delphi as the oracle of its mother Gaia before being killed by Apollo

Quiri´nus: name for the deified Romulus

Ro´mulus: son of Mars and Ilia; twin brother of Remus; founder of Rome; deified as Quirinus

Salma´cis: nymph of a pool in Caria. Loved Hermaphroditus

Sa´turn (Cro´nos): Titan son of Uranus and Gaia; father of Jupiter, Juno, Neptune, and Pluto; god of agriculture

Scyl´la: daughter of Nisus, the king of Megara. Betrayed her father and country to Minos

Sem´ele: mother of Bacchus by Jupiter; daughter of Cadmus

Sile´nus: elderly satyr; foster father of Bacchus

Sis´yphus: thieving son of Aeolus; sentenced to continually push a stone up a hill in Hades, only to have the stone always roll back down

Sy´rinx: Arcadian nymph, pursued by Pan, transformed into reeds Pan made into a panpipe

Tan´talus: son of Jupiter; father of Pelops and Niobe; served the gods his butchered son for a meal; sentenced to stand in a stream without the ability to quench his perpetual thirst

Tarpei´a: a Vestal virgin who betrayed Rome to the Sabines, who then killed her

Tar´tarus: the underworld; the infernal regions beneath Hades

Tel´amon: Argonaut, son of Aeacus; brother of Peleus and half-brother of Phocus; father of Ajax and Teucer

Te´reus: Thracian king and deceitful husband of Procne; father of Itys. Raped Philomela

Te´thys: sea goddess, wife of Oceanus

The´mis: Greek goddess of law and justice, daughter of Uranus and Gaia

The´seus: son of Aegeus; father of Hippolytus; hero of the Isthmus. Killed the Minotaur

Tire´sias: Theban son of the nymph Chariclo; father of Manto; a famous prophet

Tmo´lus: a mountain in Lydia, associated with the god of the same name

Tri´ton: sea god, half-fish son of Neptune. The sound of his horn calms or stirs up the sea

Typhoe´us: serpent-headed giant, son of Tartarus and Gaia; destroyed by Jupiter's lightning while attempting to overthrow the gods and was buried beneath Sicily

Ve´nus (Aphrodi´te, Cythere´a): goddess of love; daughter of Jupiter and Dione; wife of Vulcan; mother of Cupid and Aeneas

Vertum´nus: an Etruscan shape-changing god of fertility. Wooed Pomona

Ves´ta: goddess of the hearth fire; brought from Troy to Rome

Vul´can (Hephaes´tus): son of Juno and husband of Venus; lame god of fire and metalworking

Zeph´yrus: the West Wind